# UNBOUND II
# CHANGED WORLDS

UNBOUND II – CHANGED WORLDS
EDITED BY MJ MOORES

*Science Fiction and Fantasy Publications*
http://scififantasypublications.com
An imprint of DAOwen Publications



Unbound II – Changed Worlds
Edited by MJ Moores

ISBN 978-1-928094-21-0
EISBN 978-1-928094-19-7



Jacket art: MMT Productions

10 9 8 7 6 5 4 3 2 1

# Editor's Note

Unbound II: Changed Worlds is and will always remain an *opportunity*–for the many and varied authors to share their distinct voices; for the reader to delve into a collection of micro-worlds and explore new writers in the genre; and for me, the editor, to reconnect to my roots and share my expertise with "good storytelling" to nurture and encourage and witness the change from concept to chrysalis to final creation.

As a former postsecondary Creative Writing student, and English teacher, I was thrilled to read so many submissions that crossed the gamut of possibility within the SFF genre. This anthology not only embraces the theme of Changed Worlds but the many avenues and perspectives that make science fiction and fantasy so great. Here, you'll bear witness to the depths of future life-or-death space missions to humorous post-apocalyptic urban fantasy. These stories bring unique perspectives from an entire change in population, all the way down to the impact a seemingly innocuous event can have on one person's world outlook.

As a life-long reader, I now invite you to fall into (and perhaps a little in love with) the characters and their ever-changing worlds.

MJ Moores, OCT
Editor

# Hail Bruce

Michael Healy

The red hues of the early morning sun burnt their way through my windshield. I continued my brave battle against the relentless forces of time: bitterly holding my eyelids down just to spite the sky fire. I might have won out against the sun if a tiny but persistent rapping upon the same useless glass pane hadn't distracted me. I slipped one eye open, just enough that the sun barged through my fearsome defences and dragged me to wakefulness.

Forced to let the morning take me, I looked outside for the source of the disruption. A tiny blue bird sat perched upon my hood, leaning forward every few seconds to knock its dull beak against the windshield.

A Tweet.

Reluctantly, I rolled down my window and let the bird flutter inside. It planted itself on my dashboard and spoke in a voice not its own.

"Greetings Alex Sanders, I am the High Priest of the Temple of Bruce. Word has spread of your great deeds, and we require your aid. A few hours drive down Highway 21 will see you to our hospitality in the Bruce capitol, King's Card, where we will provide you with food and gas. Business shall be discussed then."

"I … uh …" I mumbled, as my not quite awake brain attempted to formulate a response. Not that it mattered of course, since the damned thing burst into brilliant blue flames the moment I opened my mouth, its character count exceeded. What good was a message you couldn't reply to?

I couldn't really afford to pass up a free meal, even if it did come from lunatics like the Church of Bruce. With a pained sound, half-way between a yawn and a groan, I got out of the van. Less annoyed by the early morning sun was Francis. His crimson scales absorbed the heat as he slept soundly on the van's roof, smoke escaping from his nostrils with each breath released.

"Time to get up, buddy," I said nudging the hound-sized dragon.

His little lizard body squirmed but showed no signs of waking. I reached into the cooler in the back seat and produced a raw Brachio steak. Wafting the aroma of the bloody meat toward him caused a little more stirring. Slapping it down in front of him got even more of a response.

The dragon's eyes immediately snapped open and his fangs sank deeply into the meat. A vibrant red glow flooded Francis's mouth as he cooked his meal with each bite. Lucky bastard. He gets a perfectly broiled steak every morning, while I'm stuck with old cockatrice jerky and dried berries in between jobs.

"You ready for a job?" I asked, as he swallowed the last dragon-sized bite. Francis responded by rolling on his back, and shooting a small flare's worth of flame into the air.

"Yeah, well you're almost out of meat. You'll have to kill something soon. So you might as well kill stuff that'll keep us in gas," I chastised the rebellious reptile.

Francis snarled at me but fluttered his almost comically tiny wings and jumped to the ground. I opened the door letting him in. Evidently not fast enough though, since he gave me another impatient growl while jumping inside.

Highway 21 lived up to its name only in historical value. It had seen neither pavement nor snow plow since my father was a kid. Nowadays, it was a bumpy collection of potholes and black gravel that had once been potholes. As far as the van was concerned, it was little better than the bush, if only, because it tended to lack in large trees.

The occasional sapling sprouting from a crack might grow in the months since the last time someone insane enough to fight nature out in the open happened by. Nothing I couldn't handle, of course.

Despite his previous protests, Francis slept soundly beside me while we crudely bounced from bump to bump. As we cruised a particularly flat stretch of road, I afforded myself the luxury of taking one hand from the wheel. I scratched his belly. He growled a soft little growl. Really more of a purr but I'd never insult him by saying that out loud.

I suppose compared to some monsters he was spoiled rotten. Not every hunter would feed his monster the prime cuts of a hunt or let him ride in the front seat. Heck, I could name some people who didn't treat livestock that well. He returned the favour though.

The road twisted its bumpy way toward King's Card, home of the Bruce Temple; where the loyal worshippers basked in the warmth and light of Bruce's power behind the fence while the rest of us fought to squeeze out enough food and fuel to get through the winter.

As I approached the fence, a young woman stopped me. She carried a joined pair of ancient metal tubes, the holy weapon of Bruce, a *shoutgone*. Her eyes hid behind dark lenses. She rapped her knuckles against my window until I rolled it down.

"What brings you to King's Card, Grandpa?"

Kids these days, I was barely old enough to be her father. *Grandpa*, that was just insulting. "I got a Tweet. The High Priest has a job for me."

"That's impossible. We don't hire outsiders on church business," her venomous tone wrapped around a nice little bushel of fear. It was clear, she didn't want me there.

"Maybe it's a personal matter then. All I know is I had his monster in my van telling me that there was food and gas if I braved the Highway," I rolled my eyes. "So, open the gate, or I'm driving right on through."

She shook her head but pulled the gate aside and let me in. "Drive right to the temple. Don't stop along the way. The congregation doesn't trust outsiders,"

"I wasn't planning on it," I muttered and drove by.

King's Card was just as the stories said: Long rows of houses, some hundreds of years old; Each one full of the soft, warm light of their God. Not so much as a stuttering generator to be seen or heard. I am not a religious man; been too busy trying to hold onto this life to worry about the next one. Prayer doesn't put food on the table after all: but the Church of Bruce seemed to have something to show for their faith.

The hollow towers of the Temple of Bruce loomed above my van. From the large holes, divine wrath in the form of dark, shifting smoke spewed forth. Distracted by the chemical spectacle above, I didn't see the man in the ceremonial white coat approach.

"Alex Sanders, I presume?"

"I am. You the High Priest?" Francis's eyes sprung open and he turned to the window. Smoke, darker than what the temple produced, bellowed from his nose. "Francis! Calm down!"

"I'm just his aide," the man said, stepping away from the van. His hand reached into his coat for an unseen weapon. "Your monster doesn't care for strangers?"

I grabbed Francis by the collar, pulling him away from the window. Reluctantly he backed off, letting his smoke dissipate. "He's usually better than this. Something is irritating him,"

"The Temple can have that effect on monsters not trained for it." He lowered his arms. Whatever it was he'd been reaching for he decided it wasn't important enough to waste on us quite yet.

"Your God not fond of monsters?" I asked, opening the car door and stepping out. I tightly wrapped Francis' squirming frame in my arms.

The aide shook his head as he held the temple door open for me. "Not at all. Bruce loves the monsters. They are very important to our work here."

Dwarfed by the towers and the offices sitting in the immense shade, hundreds of acolytes scurried about to fulfil any number of mundane tasks that kept the temple alive and the power flowing.

"The High Priest's office is down this hall."

I nodded my thanks and walked along the harshly lit passage. For all Bruce's seeming power, you'd think he'd spare his clergy the same soft yellow light of his flock. Not the cold-burning, sinister humming, tubes that lined the roofs of his Temple.

I walked up to the door with *High Priest* etched into the wood. I moved to knock, when I heard a commotion from within. I stopped to listen, sometimes it's good to know about your boss' problems before taking their jobs.

"You hired an outsider?" A female voice I recognized demanded—the woman who greeted me at the fence.

A second voice answered, the elderly man from the Tweet, "Your father went down there weeks ago; I am not wasting another knight when Grey is full of disposable mercenaries."

"It's always nice to feel appreciated," I gave them both my most charming smile as I entered the room. They didn't have to like me, just as long as the gas flowed my way when their monster troubles died down.

The High Priest accompanied his ritual white coat with a thick pair of rubber gloves. Even with those bulky things the shaking of his aged hands was clearly noticeable. The young woman glared at me for a moment, contempt swirling behind her eyes.

Without looking back at the High Priest, she stormed off snarling, "This isn't over!"

"It was over before it started, young lady!" The old man yelled after her, then he turned to size me up. Francis squirmed his way out of my arms, fell to the floor, and resumed his growling.

"He doesn't like it when people insult his master," I lied. Whatever bothered him about the Temple was something more than rude clergy. Not that the Priest needed to know that.

"It's hardly an insult that I do not want to throw Bruce's followers away, when I can just pay you to throw your life away." An insincere smile crossed his face, spreading wide from ear to ear.

I scratched Francis on the top of his head as I sized up the High Priest. He was lucky to be born into the safety and comfort of King's Card. His scrawny frame wouldn't have served him well where his God had no power. Although, there was a certain cunning hiding behind his eyes. He might be weak, but he was not soft. He'd be all too happy to watch me die for the glory of Bruce. There was no point in arguing with a man who only recognized me as a *person* in the broadest sense.

"What's the job?"

"The rituals to earn Bruce's blessing occur in deep catacombs beneath the Main Temple." He drew a gloved finger across blueprints on the wall. "Every so often a wild monster slips through our defences and gets into the catacombs. That's why we have knights, to take care of them."

"Something bigger got through and is killing the knights now?" It was suspect, the fence should have kept all but the biggest monsters out, and those wouldn't hide underground when there was a town to ransack. Of course, people rarely tell you the truth about how they let a dangerous monster cross into their town lines.

The High Priest nodded. "We don't know what kind of monster it is nor how something so powerful got inside the fence unseen."

Francis closed his eyes and curled up by my feet. I stroked him under the chin; at least he stopped growling. "I charge three litres an hour plus supplies. That includes any medical expenses Francis or I may incur,"

"Agreeable terms. You have a deal," He held out a hand wrapped in black rubber for me to shake.

I ignored it, and gave my final condition, "I also keep what I kill."

"Not this time. Its body belongs to the Temple." His hand dropped as he shook his head.

I took a step forward, forcing my presence upon his personal space. "I depend on these hunts for food on the road, you'll need to reimburse me."

He didn't seem at all concerned with my sudden closeness. "Five litres an hour."

"It took me three hours to get here, and it'll take another twelve to get anywhere else with people desperate enough to pay someone to kill monsters for them. Seven litres."

He ground his teeth. "Five and a week's worth of knight's rations. There are plenty of other people crazy enough to hunt monsters for me."

I cracked a slight smile, in spite of myself. He had me there. "You got a deal."

The next morning, after a reasonable breakfast courtesy of the Temple's well-stocked cafeteria, I sorted through the small armoury in the back of my van. Unidentified monsters were never pleasant to deal with. You never know what to bring with you. The wrong weapon could get you killed.

"I think we got off on the wrong foot yesterday. I'm Donna." Without any other sound, the girl appeared behind me. She sounded much too happy for someone who just lost her father.

"That's nice. I'm not taking you with me," I said, no taking my head away from the dilemma of my armaments.

"Is it because I'm a girl?" Her predictable retort dropped the pretence of joy, as fast as it had picked it up.

Forcing myself to turn around and face her I said, "No, I'm sure you're a great squire and know your way around that *shoutgone* of yours far better than I ever could. The issue is, I don't know you. I don't know how you fight, and frankly, I don't trust you to have my back. Francis and I know each other, and can look out for our weak spots. You'd just throw us off trying to look out for yours."

That caught her off guard. She stood there speechless for a moment. Once the moment passed, her eyes steeled with indignant determination. "Please, my father's down there."

"I hate to tell you this kid, but wild monsters rarely leave survivors. Especially if they're trapped with no other food in a locked tunnel." I turned back around to my weapons. "If you want to help, tell me what weapons your dad used."

She heard the implied sentiment of *so I don't make the same mistakes* but she didn't do anything more than make a slight face. "Winchester Model 1200 pump action shotgun–"

"English, I don't speak ancient weaponry," I cut her off; I assumed that was the proper name for a *shoutgone* but I didn't want to risk not knowing and taking something that got the last guy killed. "So, his shoutgone. What else?"

"Two daggers and a bullwhip." She pointed to my own versions of the weapons.

"Sounds like it's armoured or skeletal," I mused, while reaching into my shelves to produce a quarterstaff and crossbow. Francis ran circles around my feet taking flaming snaps at thin air in his excitement. He knew what the weapons meant. He knew he was going for that hunt I promised him yesterday.

Donna glanced up at me above the dark lenses. Her eyes contained a deep-seated sadness. If I had to guess, this wasn't the first time she'd lost family. "I can watch my own back."

"We aren't having this conversation. I'm not taking you with me. End of story." Francis yipped as he pranced around our feet. He seemed to like Donna, a lot more than he liked the rest of the pious residents of King's Card.

She refused to look at me as we walked back toward the Temple, her eyes flipping back and forth between the cracked pavement and Francis.

"I'm sorry kid. It's just a matter of safety. Don't take it personally."

"Whatever." She continued to stare at the loose chunks of asphalt.

I wanted to help but I barely knew her. What else could I have done?

# Hail Bruce

We walked the rest of the way draped in silence. Without words or even eye contact, she led me toward a small circular door embedded in the pavement. She bent down and pulled at the heavy wheel lock. The hidden mechanisms groaned as they spun open.

"I mean it. I don't want to see you down there," I said, disappearing with Francis into the tunnels.

The passageways were lit by the same harsh, white tubes as the Temple. Under its bleaching light the stray blood stains looked like nothing more than mud dragged in on the Priests' boots.

Francis ran in circles around me, licking the air, tasting it for traces of the other monster, as we walked past countless doors and corridors. It seemed as though this would go on forever when Francis abruptly jerked his head down a corridor and dashed off. I drew my crossbow and chased after him.

He growled defiantly at a large silver door at the end of the hall. A torn sign labelled it "*BRUCE A 1 Reactor*". Whatever had done this did so from within that room, evident from the large outward dent, almost to the point of cracking. I knocked my fist against the door; the metallic echo told me it was pure metal. I swallowed hard and stepped into the room.

The reactor comprised of an immense network of blood-stained machines. An intricate labyrinth of twisting pipes, valves, and panels covered in dials measuring all sorts of arcane details beyond my understanding. The same mechanical parts that make up my van, but on an unimaginably large scale.

An immense pool, filled with what appeared to be blood, sat in the centre of the room encompassed by the vast array of machines. Francis circled the tank, snarling at its general vileness.

Upon closer inspection, I saw steam rise from the pool as the foul liquid bubbled and boiled, causing large fleshy chunks to float about the surface without direction. "Come on Francis, it's just a sacrificial pit or something. The monster isn't there."

Francis refused to move. Stubbornly he planted himself in front of the grisly tub with a smokey snort. I took another look, not seeing anything.

"You smell something in the pit, don't you?"

Francis roared his assertion. He smelled another monster in that tank and wasn't going to move on until he had a chance to kill it. "Alright, but it's too hot for me so …"

As I spoke a small ribcage bounced up to the top of the boiling concoction. Reaching my staff into the liquid I hoisted the little thing out and dropped it to the floor. An oversized skull, almost the size of my own, sat on top of the skeleton of an infant: the body of a monster, a kobold or a large pixie, there was so little left it was hard to tell.

I picked it up and looked at the tiny bones, despite just coming out of scalding hot blood it remained cool to the touch. The meat and marrow boiled right off leaving nothing but crumbling skeleton. As I ran my fingers over the unnaturally cold bones it crumbled into dust.

What exactly monsters are had been a source of confusion for decades, since they first showed up fifty-odd years ago. Overnight the world became overrun by monsters of myth and legend. Leave it to humans to adapt to this brave new world by weaponizing the little, and not so little, beasties.

"As creepy as this is, I don't think this little guy is what's got the priests all spooked. Come on, let's go."

Francis growled a vague agreement as he walked ahead down the numbingly lit hallway. Whatever unholy secrets were used to make those tube lights was probably tied to that vat with the kobold in it. Two such horrific things in such close proximity couldn't be a coincidence.

Was that Bruce's deep dark secret? That in exchange for electricity, light, heat, safety, and comfort he demanded they slaughter monsters in his name? It'd make for more interesting services than most churches at the very least. Really, it was no different than what I did, killing monsters and using the remains; but somehow it seemed colder, more cruel. Could that little impish monster have really hurt anyone?

A metallic clank followed a thunderous bang in another room farther down the seemingly endless hall–the sound of a *shoutgone.*

"Donna …"

Francis took off in fruitless pursuit, dashing down the hallway with a vengeful snarl. Between distance and terrible acoustics, it was impossible to guess which room it had come from, even with his dragon ears. As I chased after my companion, I knew the kid would be on her own, for now at least.

Another shout echoed. It sounded closer, a good sign. Of course, it also meant the monster took the first shout and was still dangerous, a less good sign. I slowed down, ready for another sign to give me a clue where she'd gotten herself trapped. Francis seemed to have a good idea and scratched at another steel door.

I threw the slab of metal open to see Donna brandishing her shoutgone over top a bloody pile of what used to be a large monster. Whatever that monster had been was impossible to guess with mangled layers of meat wrapped around irregular bones. Donna did a number on it. She looked up at me and smirked.

"So much for needing someone to watch my back."

"You got lucky." I shrugged. Since the danger seemed to have passed on with the monster, I took a moment to survey the room we were in. It was another "Reactor" with identical machinery surrounding another boiling blood pit. "What are you doing down here?"

"You're just mad you're not getting paid." She gave me another smug expression of self-satisfied over-confidence. Francis contented himself by sniffing at the corpse, happy to let the people talk while he investigated the deceased monster.

"Then how about some answers?" I walked over to the boiling vat of former monsters. The gore from her kill or the putrid smell of the vat didn't seem to phase Donna in the least. This conversation could just as easily have taken place upstairs in the Temple cafeteria for the casual way she carried herself.

"About what?"

I always hated it when people played dumb, particularly about something starring both of us in the face. The horned equine skull of a unicorn floated to the surface for a moment before the bubbling current pushed it away again.

"That thing didn't get down here on its own. Your father brought it down here to be a sacrifice to Bruce."

"Yeah. So? Why does it matter? Point is I blew that monster back to Hell before it could kill anyone else," she replied already losing interest. She had no more reason to be in the tunnels.

"I don't like being lied to about a job." I stared into the crimson pool.

"Whatever, if it'll make you feel better. Help me carry it to reactor A 4 and I won't tell anyone you didn't kill it. Okay?" Not at all where I planned on taking the conversation, but I couldn't afford to not to get paid. I needed the gas to get far away from the King's Card as soon as possible after this.

Francis growled disapproval as Donna and I picked up the corpse and carried it down the hallway. He moaned every step of the way, as though he was afraid of what we were doing.

"Shut the lizard up! Please!" Donna said between rolling her eyes and desperate attempts to kick Francis without getting caught.

Even I was getting a little annoyed. The monster was already dead. There was nothing for him to be worried about. "That's enough Francis!"

He whimpered but complied, silently fuming little puffs of smoke as we went farther down the hall. Without the sad dragon's pleading, the silence became overly apparent. So, I brought up some small talk.

"How many of those Reactor things do you got anyways?"

"Eight. Four here and four more in another facility down the street," Donna explained utterly disinterested.

"Eight? How many monsters do you need?" Even awkward disinterested conversation was better than the distrusting silence we had going.

"I don't know. We send out hunting parties every few months, they bring home two hundred or so and it gets us by." She shrugged a bit not seeming to care.

I'm lucky if I get that many monsters a year. That many every few months is absurd. It's a wonder there were monsters in Bruce County at all. I had nothing to possibly add to this until we reached the Reactor room. "Here we are. Let's go."

The horrific array of machinery and the grisly sacrificial pit were beginning to lose their impact on me. So much horror in such a short time just kind of numbs the mind. Watching an unidentifiable exoskeleton of some insect monster bob with the splitting bubbles, I said, "So, what now?"

"Just drop it in. Bruce will handle the rest." She shrugged as she casually tossed her half into the pool.

Francis whimpered again as I followed suit and let my half of the corpse fall into the boiling mix of putrid monster meat. As the corpse fell into the slurry, the boiling ceased. For a moment, the blood stopped all movement, siting as tranquil as an isolated pond.

A solid mass of meat rose up from the pool. Stepping back, Donna reached for her *shoutgone*.

"What the Hell?"

I drew my staff and knocked the large monster out of the vat with a sideways swing. Away from the other remains of monsters, the creature rolled onto its four legs, silently snarling an expansive jaw full of stolen teeth.

"It's a Rawhead. A scavenger that expands its body with stolen parts from other creatures."

"Like two dozen dead monsters in a vat?" Her skin lost colour as rapidly as her voice lost confidence. The Rawhead charged Donna, not remotely bothered by the shout from the *shoutgone*.

"Yeah, that's not a good combination," I said overtop a chain of largely useless roars ringing out from the *shoutgone*. Donna didn't acknowledge me though, either because she couldn't hear me or she was busy trying to back away from a hundred kilograms of fanged death.

It slowed as it backed her into a corner and opened its mouth as though trying to roar without vocal cords. Donna triggered another shout, but the weapon just let out a feeble click. She dropped it.

As the monster reared its ugly pig-shaped face over the girl, preparing to snap its mismatched jaw down on her herd, Francis charged forward planting his teeth firmly into the Rawhead's leg.

The beast cried out in silent pain as it quickly turned around to confront the little dragon, still digging sharpened teeth into its back heel.

Francis stalwartly held his toothy grip on the leg, letting his interior heat surge into his mouth. The meat blackened as Francis charred the Rawhead's appendage.

Safely ignored, Donna dropped to the ground and reached for her *shoutgone*. Madness in my eyes, as the weapon had already proved useless and seemed to be broken now. As long as she was safe though, I left her to her own devices. Francis and I would have to take care of this monster ourselves.

I stepped forward with my staff in hand and swung it down onto the Rawhead's back. The wood shattered into splinters as it made contact. What little meat it did displace gave way to reveal the same sort of exoskeleton that had floated in the tank.

Slamming its hind leg, and Francis, into the wall the Rawhead successfully forced the dragon to relinquish his grasp. The burnt meat flaked away to reveal nothing but standard looking bone, the exoskeleton didn't go that far down the Rawhead's body.

Francis laid on the ground, dazed from the impact. The Rawhead turned its attention to me. I reached for my crossbow but knew it wasn't going to help much. I had one bolt loaded, and that alone couldn't put down a monster this size even without stolen armour.

As it stalked toward me, careful not to put too much pressure on its wounded hind leg, it extended cat like claws on its front feet. Intending to rend me apart with those oversized blades, it dove forward.

I rolled to the side behind a tangled mess of pipes that caught the claws for me. Where the claws struck the steel it gave way, creating large cracks in the pipes. Steam and hot water flowed onto the Rawhead causing it to back off for a moment.

On the other side of the room, Donna had her *shoutgone* split apart and was shoving tiny bronze cylinders into the weapon. Francis stirred where the Rawhead had left him by the wall. Taking my brief moment of safety, I thought of a plan.

"Francis! Distraction!"

Even dazed by blunt impact, Francis heard the order and breathed a short stream of flame at the Rawhead. At that distance, it wasn't very hot, barely scorching the monster's flesh, but it was enough to turn its back on me and focus on the young dragon.

Taking advantage of Francis' diversion, I crawled beneath the pipes toward Donna. She slammed her weapon back together, apparently finished with is repairs.

"Do you know how the sacrificial vat works?" I yelled.

Francis ducked under the Rawhead, hiding for a moment in the safety of his own foe's underbelly, where claws and fangs couldn't reach. He clamped down on some meat, and ripped it free without even using flame. The Rawhead tried to roar again as it desperately shuffled its body to reach the smaller monster hiding underneath.

Donna nodded frantically. I smiled and pointed at the pipes.

"It'll take more than just water to break down a monster corpse. Which pipe has the–"

"Hydroflouric acid, that one there." She pointed to a pipe perfectly placed right over top of the Rawhead.

"Is your *shoutgone* fixed?"

She nodded at me despite a slightly confused look. I laughed a little in spite of myself.

"Francis! Amscram!"

Hearing the order, Francis bolted, running with all the force his little lizard limbs could offer, away from the enemy monster.

Holding back another triumphant laugh I yelled, "Shout at the pipe."

Donna aimed her weapon at the pipe and fired another roar. Holes burst into the pipe pouring the acid upon the angry Rawhead. It continued its horrified, silent screams as the clear liquid burned through all of its stolen meat, leaving nothing but a disjointed collection of assorted bones wrapped around the skeleton of a harmless pig.

Eventually, the acid flow stopped as someone above noticed the rapid loss in pressure. Donna fell to her knees, muttering her thanks to Bruce, begging his forgiveness for destroying his alter. I just leaned against the wall and scratched Francis under the chin.

We were done here.

"I took the liberty of having the gas and food loaded into your van while you were down there," The High Priest said as he greeted us outside the hatch.

"Thanks, just make sure your knights are more careful about what they toss in the vats next time and you'll be fine," I muttered and watched him sputter speechlessly. "Also, don't be too hard on the kid. She'll make a good knight in a few years if you let her."

He stared at me blankly as I walked away for a moment before the hatch opened again and Donna stepped out. I could almost hear his scolding all the way back to the van. I was tempted to wait around and see what he was going to do, but my job here was done. Time to get back on the road.

Michael Healy was born in Toronto, Ontario but currently makes his home in the much colder Owen Sound, Ontario with his wife and her senile cat. Raised on a steady diet of superheroes, fantasy and science fiction from young childhood he was shaped into a writer from a young age. You can find his work in Urban Green Man, Superhero Monster Hunter: The Good Fight. Follow him on twitter @MichaelHealy18

# Reclaiming the Elements

By Daniel Powell

Five weary men stepped out from beneath the shadows and into the light. For more than a month they'd tread lightly through the Watchful Woods, a forest so dense that in places they blazed torches in the noon hour.

"So, my lord," said Arven Grem, "I trust it's a familiar sight?"

"Of course," Prince Baylon Fielding replied. "How could I forget the playfields of my childhood?"

"Childhood!" The squat man with the gruff voice laughed. "You're little more than a boy as we stand here, my lord! And playfields? Gah! That's the first time I'd ever heard Meadow Red saddled with *that* one."

The prince smiled at his companion—not unkindly. No insult was intended. Indeed, what could insults mean anymore to men in their *condition*?

They had departed Harrow Colony in early spring, just days after sowing the rock-strewn fields for their meager summer harvest. Now, standing at long last in sight of the Greentower, the frigid air stung their lungs. Six inches of ice-crusted snow covered Meadow Red, and the ground crunched beneath their boots as they headed for the castle.

"Raise the standards," Baylon said. "And pray to the Grays who protect us that we won't fall again today."

While the men shared an ashen tone of skin, only one bore minimal outward signs of the injury that had killed him. Scarred, stitched, burned, and speared were four in the company, but Baylon appeared almost as he did the day of his passing—aside, of course, from the indigo stains on his lips, the signature of the scornroot which had brought a great and proud culture so much bitter sorrow over these last years.

Two of the men unfurled the standards of Harrow Colony–a white, half-risen sun over a black field littered with bones; a third flew a simple purple scarf on the biting winds. Even here, at the northern edge of the Brittle Continent, it was still recognized as the universal sign for peaceful conference.

"Halt." Baylon pressed a hand to Grem's chest. "We'd best venture no farther. One way or another, they'll send forth an emissary."

No sooner had the words left his lips than a warning arrow pierced the ground, twenty paces before them. Baylon swallowed thickly. He glanced at his strategist; the little man shrugged and offered a faint smile, a hint of the stitching scars that had closed the second smile in his neck barely visible above his breastplate.

Meadow Red remained still and quiet; the only sounds made were the winds barreling off the Aisle of Spouting Horns and out across the clearing, carrying with them whispers of salt and blood, of the indomitable sea and fallen men. There was a thunderous din–the seldom-opened front gates creaking wide in the distance–and then a phalanx of riders on muscular Fielding Stallions coming forth at a brisk trot.

They wore full armor, and were heavily armed. Baylon smiled. Even though he knew the tower watchmen had already relayed the impossible news to his father, his family still took every necessary precaution. And, of course, they were wise in doing so. The world had changed in the last decade, and one could never be too careful in such trying times.

A light snow fell as the riders approached. Baylon and his men waited in the chill, understanding that the setting sun and the freezing wind spelled doom for them all if they could not quarter in Greentower. There would be no return to the Arborist's cottage–no safe passage back to Harrow Colony. Winter held the Ice Barons in its grip, and the Watchful Woods were no port in the storm.

No, for them it would either be Greentower or a return to the long and troubled sleep.

Baylon's smile grew as the king's men approached. *Good for Father!* He had continued Brenton's military education in his absence, and clearly the king felt comfortable enough to send the lad with his most trusted guards.

"Whoa," Brenton said, bringing the company to a halt. The men in his father's guard were skilled warriors–experienced with iron and hale with muscle. Brenton, on the other hand, remained slight and lean. At just sixteen years of age, he still did not possess the marks of battle or the bruises of politics that made men suspicious and cruel.

He removed his helmet, his blond hair cropped close to the skull in the way of the Fieldings. He swallowed hard and, in one fluid motion, dismounted.

"Lord Brenton," Killney Scarton, his sworn sword, said. "It's not wise to approach them. Orders are to simply to escort them to the–"

"It's okay, Killney," Brenton said. He tucked his helmet away, walked rapidly across the crusted snow, falling instantly into Baylon's open arms without a second thought.

"Brother," he whispered, a tear streaking his cheek as he stared into Baylon's eyes. "You've come *back* to us!"

"Aye. I surely have, Brent. And it's a blessing to see *you*, my brother, now so tall and strong. Now so grown up. Tell me–how is Father?"

Brenton stepped away from his brother's embrace. He stared into his eyes, searching for something–anything *off*–before breaking into a stunned smile.

"They said you were *dead*. They said … they said you were put to rest in the heathen tombs beneath the Ballack Dunes. How did you ever make it through the Watchful Woods?"

Baylon laughed. He squeezed his brother's shoulder as the boy finally took the measure of his traveling companions. Brenton grimaced in confusion as he finally noticed the scars, the missing eye, and the burns.

"We lack the *vital elements*," Baylon said simply. "And so, the watchers could not detect our passing. In that way, you might surmise that some part of us is still dead. The great Master Viskul will be none too pleased when he learns how we penetrated his defenses."

"Oh, well *that's* a given," Brenton said with a chuckle. "He'll hold your feet to the fire on that account for sure, the old sourpuss. Come, Brother. There is room enough for your"–he cleared his throat–"for your men, of course. Our parents are eager to see if–if any of this is real."

"And what about you? What do you think? Is this–are *we*–real?"

Brenton pulled his brother into a second embrace.

"Of course, dear brother. Of course. You've come *back* to us, and I'd know the light in your eyes from behind a thousand close helmets. Now come … please. Father is waiting, and the night draws near."

The Hall of the Dozens stretched three stories toward the heavens. The greatest in all of the Ice Barons, it had been built by Annaston Fielding, Handbreaker of the Hills and First Lord of the Green Mountains. His statue sat at the apex of the upper chamber, the wise king's visage peered down on the royal thrones. Twelve granite statues of Fielding kings graced each of the upper stories. Eleven more ringed the periphery of the ground floor, with Baylon's grandfather's statue mere steps from where his mother and father now sat. Thornton Fielding had been gone nine years, and Baylon still held fond memories of ice fishing with him; the old man sometimes offering him a nip of the spirits he kept in the horn around his neck.

A simple granite dais awaiting the immortalization of the present king, the mighty Freighton Fielding, stood behind the thrones. It was always there, that stone dais, and its very presence was enough to keep the Lords of Greentower sharp in their rule.

Known throughout the Brittle Continent as Lord Thunderclap, Freighton Fielding was broad in the shoulder and wrist, and firm in his honor and judgment. Though graying, he still bore the trappings of his youth–the strength and the charisma ever-present in his smile and kind granite eyes.

He sat on Arbixus, the great throne of the Ice Barrons, carefully scrutinizing the figure now standing before him. How Baylon resembled the son he had lost on the far side of the world!

"Who *are* you?" The king gripped the arms of his throne so hard his knuckles matched the color of the snow falling outside. It was all the man could do to keep his hands from shaking.

"I am Baylon Fielding, firstborn son of Lord Thunderclap, the King of the Ice Barons and protector of the Great Peace. I am also known as Baylon the Risen, firstborn son of an honorable queen and eldest brother and protector of the princes and princess of Greentower. Others know me as Lord Baylon the Unblemished, lord of Harrow Colony and leader of the Half Risen–the gray army of the relentless tide." He knelt before the throne, and his cohort followed him to their knees.

"I *am* Baylon Fielding," he softly continued, eyes trained on the granite floors. "Your son, returned."

"Stand," Queen Emaline said. "Please, Baylon. Stand, so I might look on you."

He rose, and she did the same from her throne, Arbixum. The queen remained striking in her beauty, all those frozen winters unable to whither the rose blossoms in her cheeks. Unlike her husband, she made no pretense of strength, her hands shaking as she descended the stairs toward her son. She took his hands and peered into his blue eyes, searching for the spark of identity only a mother can discern in the soul of her baby boy.

"Oh," she said. Her eyes filled with tears and she put a hand to her mouth in shock. "Oh … *Baylon.*"

He smiled as she extended her hand. Touching his cheek, the Queen's eyes grew wet and full, leaking tears. She traced the curve of Baylon's jaw and touched his hair at the temple.

"It's him. Freighton, it's *him*. It's our Baylon, returned to us. It's him!"

Fielding stood and clamored down the steps. Emaline pulled Baylon close, and the young man embraced his mother; she smelled of juniper. The weight of his father's hand pressed against his back.

"Son?" Baylon reached and pulled his father close to them both. "How is this possible, Baylon? They said you were killed …"

"I was." His mother's hair muffled the reply. "I *was* killed, Father. And then I was risen."

They were given quarters and baths, clean clothing and wine.

"So, *this* is how you grew up, eh?" Arven Grem said. The tall man with the broken smile had once been a Tanish Pirate, a mercenary from the barrier islands of Tane. He had met his end in Aliceport when the Saltlords sacked the city an hour before dawn. Now, he was the field general of 13,000 of the half-risen.

When they'd left Harrow Colony, Holder Brim and his priests continued raising scores from the grave. Those who would not take the oath were returned to the long and troubled sleep. And those who simply wished no part of resurrection, such as it was, were likewise dispatched a second, final time.

But most … well, most *did* want to stay and, even if their fealty to the oath was half-hearted, the great majority fell in line with what they were trying to build in Harrow Colony. Life there wasn't pretty, of course, but it certainly beat the alternative.

"Oh, nay," Baylon said with a wink, "we had it *a lot* better than this, Hai Grem. Don't forget, now–this is only the guest's quarters!"

"Ah, piss off!" Gildon Scrimshaw said. He'd been accused of spying while trading slaves in The Crags. The wasp people who lived there rearranged his features with vials of their potent venom. "Ye' might've been fancy once, *Lord* Baylon, but now we's all the same. Half risen, but *fully* obedient. Don't matter if ye' come from royalty or a bugger's squat in Lowrank."

"Aye, Gilly. Aye–you're right, and I wouldn't have it any other way. But still, and I mean no disrespect to any of you when I say this, you'll need to let me do the talking this evening. There are protocols in place when dealing with people like my father. Couple those with the shock of our very presence, and it could make for an exceedingly *interesting* meal."

"What's so shocking about our presence?" Bart Low said. He grinned and wine spilled from the corner of his ruined mouth, down his scarred cheek. He'd been called nothing but "Low" for so long he'd forgotten his birth name, but it suited him all the same. There had been no thievery since Holder Brim spoke the words over him, but the name stuck. "You afraid we'll embarrass ye' in front of all the pretty, pretty people?"

They laughed at the joke, but there existed a kernel of truth in his words. It would take finesse to deliver the message–finesse and good fortune. Baylon hated coming home under these circumstances, but what were his options? If the Brittle Realms knew about Harrow Colony, all would've been lost. They would have raised an army and squashed the relentless tide in half a day's work. It was by the grace of the Grays that his own parents had received him with such generosity of spirit.

The living, blood ties notwithstanding, didn't suffer the dead (or even the half-risen) easily.

They dressed in the clean garments of nobles and were escorted to Harmony Hall for their dinner. News of the prince's return spread quickly, and Greentower's gentry were in full attendance. The lords and ladies marveled at the young man as he passed their chairs, his hair neatly in place and a warm smile on his purple lips. The priests looked at him with awe; they grimaced at the sight of his grisly companions.

The half-risen sat at the king's hand, Baylon so close to his father he could see the deep lines near his eyes. *Had they been so pronounced when I departed for the southlands, all those stages of the moon before?*

Brenton and Mallon sat with their young sister, Amalia, between them. The princess stared unabashedly at her eldest brother, her mouth agape. She'd been but three when he'd departed for the southlands, and there was just a spark of recognition in her for the man now sitting across the table.

The king stood. He bowed and kissed his queen's hand before turning to address the gentry and his children. "The rumors are true," he said, drawing a murmur at the table. "Baylon has come home to Greentower."

Baylon stood. He offered the most assured smile he could muster and gave them a little half-bow before reclaiming his seat.

Brenton studied his older brother with wonder in his eyes. Mallon wore a sheepish grin that warmed with every passing second, the disbelief quickly losing out to the joy of having his brother home. And Amalia simply stood and boisterously clapped her hands. This act of innocent exuberance broke the tension in the room, and the place exploded with laughter.

After a time, Baylon raised a hand. "Thank you for welcoming me and my company. It's very good to be home. It's good to be with *all* of you again, although I wish it were under different circumstances." He leaned forward to maintain eye contact up and down the great table.

"My men and I have traveled across the whole of the continent to meet with you tonight. I know my very presence here is a surprise, and it's true– I *fell* there in the Southlands. I was poisoned in my chambers, a scurrilous act of war rendered by the treasonous Bendalinas."

Agitated grumbling filled the room. Quelnar Brahn, one of the few lords in the Ice Barrons that still wore his hair long, stood and pointed at Baylon with his goblet. "I killed Isaac Bendalina at the Battle of Torsh Path, Prince Fielding! His skull still decorates the mantle of my guard's chambers!"

This drew a roar of approval from the table, and those assembled clamored to speak over each other, documenting the scores of Bendalinas they'd slew and the variety of creative ways for executing their foes.

"Enough!" Freighton commanded. The room fell silent. "I have had no council on such matters with my son, but a father's intuition tells me it's not the Bendalinas that he's here to discuss. Please, Baylon. Continue."

He nodded. "I fell there in that sandy, foreign kingdom, and I was lost. The pain … I'll not forget the pain of the scornroot in all of my remaining days. I fell there, and I was put to rest in a common tomb beneath a city filled with cutthroats and mercenaries."

A single tear slid down the queen's cheek, for no sorrow is as terrible as that of a parent knowing of a child's pain and being powerless to stop it. Save the crackle of pitch in the great hall's hearth, the room stood silent.

"And then I was risen again." He nodded to his companions. "We call him Holder Brim. He is a priest of the Forgotten Aisles–a wise man who prays to the Ancient Grays. He … brought me out of the tombs beneath the Ballack Dunes and once again into the light."

This drew another round of excited murmuring. "Baylon," Emaline said when the room grew quiet, "Son … what are you telling us? Do you no longer worship the Gods of Light?"

"I respect them, Mother. I respect them with all my heart, as I always have and always will. You and Father raised me well, and I've been blessed by your influence. But in Harrow Colony–in our *home* in the Forgotten Aisles"–he shook his head–"it is true, we have other Gods. Benevolent Gods. Gods we'll need more than ever, you see, because a terrible scourge is coming. A vast and insidious blight is making its way across the deserts and over the plains of Terák-Aiht. It's a menace so vile–so dominated by corruption–that it's uncertain if *any* of our faiths can sustain us–the Ancient Grays *or* the Gods of Light."

"What is this scourge you speak of?" Freighton asked. "The Bendalinas? They've been scattered to the winds of the five continents. The price on their heads, should they dare show them in the markets of the Brittle Continent, will ensure they never set foot in the Ice Barons again."

As they spoke, servants ladled rich seafood chowder into silver bowls. Plates of cheese and fruit and great baskets of bread and fine, whipped butter worked their way up and down the table. Wine goblets were filled; molasses mead poured. A string quartet plucked a subdued hymn from a balcony near the statue of the Handbreaker.

"Not the Bendalinas, Father. If only our problems were so small. There is a ruler with a kingdom stretching at least twice the measure of the Ice Barons–a man called Xerick Khan. He rules the–"

"The Silklands of Terák-Aiht. Yes, Baylon–we know of him. He's always upheld the peace. What consequence is a farmer, albeit one who charges a king's ransom for his moth-ridden wares, from the other side of the world to the people of the Brittle Continent?"

"He's no mere farmer, King Fielding," Grem said. "Begging your pardon, sir, but the Xerick Khan you are thinking of is lost to our world. This … *creature* now amassing a great army"–Grem shook his head–"is something completely different."

"Creature? Son, why is your companion so cryptic?"

Baylon sipped his soup, choosing his words carefully. "Hai Grem speaks the truth. You see, not unlike the people of the Ice Barons, the inhabitants of the Silklands–they are called the Kotharks–worship gods of the heavens. Just as the lights of the Northlands imbue the people with strength here, the Kotharks have tethered their faith to a vast field of southern stars. Their constellations are unlike anything we've seen here on the Brittle Continent. Roughly sixteen stages ago, those constellations simply *fell apart.* Something happened in the sky, and some matter of the heavens crashed down into the deserts of Terák-Aiht."

"Bah!" Petrus Cantow said. "I've not missed a single night's watch, Prince Fielding, and I can't recall such an occurrence. Meteors and asteroids–we study them all. We should know if there was such an event!"

"I don't doubt your persistence, Hai Cantow," Baylon said. "But *these* constellations! They were unlike anything I'd ever seen before. Surely, they are not visible from anywhere on the Brittle Continent–not in *any* season. I lost sight of them on the voyage back across the sea."

Cantow conceded the point's possibility with a shrug, for he'd never been farther south than the lower Steppe. Baylon pushed on.

"I was at least two stages at sea before stepping foot on Terák-Aiht. I can only tell you, in all my time spent there, I was anxious to return home to the Brittle Continent. The rituals, the food, the way of life–all were very different there in the desert lands."

"Were they unkind to you?" Emaline asked. Bowls were slowly cleared, and servants brought plates piled high with roast hog and wine-braised vegetables.

"No, Mother. Not at all. Most Kotharks I met were quite generous–in both spirit and accommodations. I never ventured into the capital, but I did linger a few weeks in an outpost town called Dane. Dane sits on a large river that winds through the great valley of Terák-Aiht before spilling into the sea. Inside its walls, the master weavers of Terák-Aiht turn the raw silk from the southlands into some of the finest robes in all of the five continents.

"While I was there, I heard many rumors. Whispers. Fears that the sky was growing closer, and a terrible evil would visit the continent of Terák-Aiht. The people were frightened, Mother. Something made them nervous beyond reason."

Freighton speared a piece of hog and chewed on one side of his mouth while studying his son. "What are we talking about here? Magic? Sorcery?"

Baylon shrugged. "Perhaps. I can't be sure if it's sorcery, or some manifestation of true divinity. If there's one thing I've learned since

Holder Brim spoke the words over me and I opened my eyes a second time, it's that there are mysteries and wonders far beyond the ordinary scope of human thinking. All I can tell you for sure is I didn't like it on Terák-Aiht.

"I delivered the articles of the Great Peace to the proper attendants, of course. When work was finished, I left immediately and departed for the Brittle Continent. Upon my return to Fahl's Bay, my heart and instincts told me to ride hard for Greentower, but I was delayed in the halls of Courtney Way by the Bendalinas. The rest … well, the rest you know. But here's the thing, Father. Something *did* happen in the skies above Terák-Aiht, and we've got witnesses in our army who will attest to it. We sent a party of half-risen Kotharks back to Terák-Aiht, and they confirmed our fears.

"A star *did* fall from the sky, and has corrupted the people of the continent. Xerik Khan has changed, and now he's coming north. He means to end the Great Peace. The Brittle Continent is the first step in his conquest."

"And you trust these Kotharks? How do you know your scouts remain loyal to you?"

"Because they're from Harrow Colony, Hai Thunderclap," Scrimshaw said. "They can *only* serve the Colony. And the things they said–the things they told us about Khan's army …" He shook his head sadly.

The room once again fell silent. "Go ahead," Emaline said. "Speak freely, Hai–"

"Gilly Scrimshaw, Your Highness," he replied with a kindly smile. "'Tis enough to call me Gilly. They warned of an army on the march, and of rolling battlements so high they blocked the southern sun. They spoke of a mad king–a once fair and proud man made ill by the black powder. And they spoke of monsters–hideous, malformed giants from the sand kingdoms made subservient to the transformed tyrant."

"Black powder?" Freighton asked.

"The star that fell … Xerick Kahn had his men transport it back to the royal halls. Still warm, it hummed with an alien energy, King Fielding, and it shed a potent black dust. Kahn ingested it, and it made him insane. It had … other effects as well."

"Go on, Gilly." Freighton pushed his half-eaten plate away, and a servant rushed in to clear it and refill his goblet. "We're too far down the road not to have it all come out."

"He *grew*, King Thunderclap. He was always a large man, but they say now he can no longer fit inside his royal coach. No horse on the entire continent of Terák-Aiht can bear his weight. Fifty men now carry him on their shoulders such is his pride.

"He is monstrous with muscle and his mind is confused with bouts of rage and bloodlust. He …well, his appetites have changed. He no longer observes the principles of civility; it's been said that he eats the hearts of his men and enemies alike. And he is building a war machine the likes of which has never been seen; he is sacking every neighboring city he passes through and sending slave armies to the farthest edges of Terák-Aiht. And he is coming this way, sir. He knows the north is the least populated of the five continents, and it is *here* he hopes to begin his conquest."

"Why, Baylon? Why would he discard the Great Peace?" Emaline asked.

"Why does any man raise a spear against his fellow man, Mother? For power."

Servants brought strawberry tarts, but Freighton waved his off with a hand and called for spirits instead. Decanters of the royal brandy appeared, and draughts of the fine amber liquid were distributed to his council. He grew silent as the gentry spoke quietly amongst themselves, his thoughts occupied by an army on the march.

As she finished her tart, Amalia stared at her older brother with naked curiosity. "Did it hurt, Baylon?" she asked.

"Shhh, girl!" Brenton said, but Baylon simply nodded.

"Aye, Sister. It was the worst pain I've ever experienced. I did not go peacefully, dear girl. And neither will any of us if the transformed king gets a foothold on the Brittle Continent."

"But he won't," the girl replied with absolute certainty. "He *can't*."

Baylon and his men laughed.

"And why is that, my Amalia?"

"Because the protectors of the Brittle Continent won't allow it."

"Oh? And what do you know of these protectors, dear Sister?"

Faithful in her lessons, Amalia beamed. "I know Ashram fell from the sky to make the world a habitable place for his children. I know the world was a cold and desolate place before his grace, and he lit the great fires beneath Peak Ashram that split the brittle continent into realms and spread warmth through a world that had only known ice and darkness. He wouldn't forsake those who serve him faithfully here in the Ice Barons."

Emaline looked on her daughter with pride while Baylon sighed heavily. His eyes fell on his untouched dessert. She'd recited the passage like an incantation, and that's just what it had been once to him as well. The fables of Ashram the Maker held sway over the Brittle Continent, even though it was the Grays of the Southern Reach that possessed the power to restore the fallen to life.

He smiled at his sister. "You're very wise, dear girl. You can recite the words at a much younger age than I ever could."

Amalia beamed. She opened her mouth to speak but closed it abruptly when her father stood. The music ceased and Freighton drained his cup. The men in his council followed suit.

"My son has returned to Greentower. He speaks only the truth. I will dispatch a party of scouts. War is coming. We must take measures to protect the Ice Barons, if not the Brittle Continent–Gods bless us. For tonight"–he peered up and down the rows of assembled gentry–"we will celebrate Baylon's return. But tomorrow, we begin our preparations."

An old priest named Hawthorne coughed lightly and raised a hand. "Forgive me, my lord, but just what is it we make preparations *for*? A giant cannibal of the Silklands and his hoard of desert monsters? Perhaps it would be wise to await the findings of your scouts, would it not? The very act of raising a northern army could threaten an already fragile peace."

"Wise point, Hai Hawthorne, and for mentioning it, you will be excused from tonight's council. I trust the words of my son and his men. We will send the scouts as a formality only, for Kahn's hordes may already be at our doorstep in the time it takes them to cross the sea. Be gone, old man. Your meal is finished here tonight."

"But my lord, I swear to you that I meant no …" The guards took him lightly by the arms and bore him from the room.

"Brenton and Baylon, please join us. I thank the rest of you for uniting with my family in this joyous reunion, and I free you to your own homes with an oath of secrecy concerning the matters discussed here tonight. Be silent and be vigilant. Await our instructions, and stand together for the good of the Ice Barons and the Realms of the Brittle Continent."

The quartet launched into another song, and Baylon hugged his mother and youngest siblings. He followed his father and council–just four men, not counting Brenton–into the strategy chamber.

"Brandy for all," Freighton said to his attendant. They sat around the table, a map of the five continents in the center. Daniel Thickart sat at

Freighton's side. The lord of Gloam Hall on the upper Steppe, he had known Freighton Fielding since their lessons, and was his staunchest military ally in the Ice Barons. Karl Jurgens of Black Hall on the Sea controlled the largest navy on the continent, and Brūss Jornish, the horse master from Arden Glen, sat across from the Fielding boys. The fourth in his father's council was the cadaverously thin Barkwill, a priest who'd spent parts of his youth in the Watchful Woods, hiding from the seers and the wrath of Master Viskul, before taking his oaths in the seminary of Greentower.

Baylon never liked him, and he liked him even less upon his return to Greentower. The bald man had sickly, sallow skin and great shadows beneath his eyes. He looked–well, he looked *taller* somehow, his features even more grotesque. When he smiled at Baylon, his teeth flashed a hideous yellow, seeming impossibly long and sharp.

Still, he was a cunning strategist and his father's personal conduit to the Gods of Light.

"Your lips," Barkwill said, touching his own. "Will the stains fade with time?"

"They haven't yet. Perhaps when the summer sunshine returns to the Southern Reach."

"Ah, the Southern Reach," Barkwill said. "Your new and permanent home, Master Baylon?"

"Aye."

Freighton opened his mouth to protest, but Baylon beat him to the punch. "Begging your pardon, Father, but it's simply how things must be. I have a title in Harrow Colony, and a responsibility to my men. I came here only to warn you, and to pledge to you my eternal loyalty and the services of my men. Not to reclaim my life here in Greentower."

Freighton shook his head in sadness. "Baylon, your mother and I prayed to the Gods of the Northland Lights that you would return to us, and now here you sit at my strategy table, here *in the flesh*. And so, you say you will leave us a second time? You'll break your mother's heart. You understand that, don't you?"

"I do, Father, and it pains me so. But I will be your hand in the south. I will stand with the army of the relentless tide at the gates of the Reach and I will fight to the death to keep what's coming far away from Greentower. And if we prevail, I promise we will all be together again–whether it's here in Greentower or down on the shores of the Southern Reach. Distance means nothing to blood, Father, and I will always be your son."

The king smiled. "You have honored yourself and our family. I'm glad to have you home, even if it's only for a short time."

"Lord Thunderclap, who will ride?" Jornishasked, shifting the talk. "I can have a dozen of our fastest Fielding Stallions on the mark at first light."

They drank–all but Brenton–until late in the evening as they formed their plans. When the clock chimed in the new morning, Brenton retired to his chambers and the nobles left for their quarters–all but Daniel Thickart. He, Freighton, and Baylon took to the upper battlements to look out over the kingdom. Beyond the walls, Meadow Red lie still and silent, the spilled blood of Fielding kings frozen in the soil beneath the snow.

Just above the Green Mountains, a shifting band of lights danced on the horizon. Purples, blues, reds and greens–always greens.

Daniel Thickart turned to Baylon. He wore a bemused smile. "Do you know how we Thickarts took our surname, Baylon?"

The boy shook his head.

"Really? You've never heard the tale Relki Thickart, the first great lord of the Steppe? He fought the Bounty Raiders, many centuries ago. They came by sea, the raiders did, and they were furious warriors."

"They had something of a reputation," Baylon admitted. "I've heard stories. Terrible stories."

Thickart nodded before sipping his brandy. "Aye. And well deserved that reputation. Their chieftains ate the hearts of the lords they conquered. The heathens never took the Steppe, of course, but my great ancestor Relki *did* fall in battle. The story says that Alistair Thane, the very worst of the Bounty Raiders and their fiercest field general, attempted to make a meal of Relki's heart." Thickart grinned at the thought of it. He relished his drink, and Baylon saw his father smile at the story.

"What happened?" Baylon asked, drawn into the tale. He sipped the biting liquid.

"The bastard choked to death on it! Relki's heart *expanded* in his throat. By the time Thane's medical advisers reached his tents, the tyrant's gut was distended with the *beating heart* of our family forebears. They tried to cut it out of him, but there was just too much. They say Thane's bloated body was burned there on the Steppe, the beating heart of Relki Thickart still expanding inside the foolish raider king as the flames licked his corpse. All these hundreds of years, and the Steppe has never fallen. Not once."

"Thick heart," Baylon said, laughing. "I get it, now: *Thickart.*"

"Aye," Daniel said, joining him in laughter. "Thick heart indeed. Tis how some words are made, you know. They come from the truths of things. And if that cannibal silk king is truly coming to the Steppe, then he'll learn the meaning of the name for himself. I can promise you that."

The half-risen took their breakfast at the table of the queen. Freighton traveled south with his guard to see the scouts off at dawn.

They made idle chat, speaking happily of the coming holiday–Baylon twice bringing tears to his mother's eyes when he told her they were soon departing for Harrow Colony and could not celebrate Winter's Head at Greentower.

"But *why*, Son? Why must you leave?"

"My men need me, Mother. It's not a simple thing for me, either, to leave the family I love with all of my heart for a second time. You have to understand that. But I have responsibilities now. The whole of the Brittle Continent needs me–not just Greentower. War is coming and I will be the first to meet it."

Amalia and Mallon picked at their breakfast, saddened by news of their brother's departure.

"When the weather turns," he said, hoping to change the subject, "then perhaps the three of you can visit me in the south."

"In that terrible place?" Mallon said, making a face. "An entire *city* filled with the dead? No thanks, Baylon."

"Mallon!" Emaline hissed at her youngest son. "You be respectful to our guests."

"No offense taken," Gilly Scrimshaw said, fingering a knob of scarred flesh on his neck. "Except with the term 'dead.' Not particularly appropriate for men in our condition any longer."

"So then, what *are* you?" Amalia said.

"I told you, Sister. We're *half*-risen."

"Why only half, Son? You appear whole in my eyes."

Baylon shrugged. "Holder Brim said there's something in the blood we lack. He calls it the 'Vital Elements'. But he believes there's a chance for full restoration."

"What would that do, Baylon? What's missing?"

"We … can't love the way we once did," Grem interjected. "We'll have no children. No families. That's why we're so bound to each other on Harrow Colony. But Holder Brim–he's close to unlocking the rest. He's close to restoring us as full men–by the grace of the Grays."

Emaline thought about this in silence for a long time. "And that … that's how you slipped through the forest?"

Baylon nodded. "But we're not half-dead, Mother. Far from it. We're closer than ever to life, and we're here to serve the Brittle Continent. We're here to serve you and Father."

As if on cue, a knock sounded on the door of the queen's chambers. Master Viskul entered the room, his thick robes collecting in a pile on his arched back. "So ye' slipped right through, did ye'? *Damn* the Gods …"

"Master Viskul!" Emaline said. "There are *children* present!"

"Begging your pardon, M' Lady. I'm old, and have forgotten my manners. May I?"

She nodded warily, and the old man took coffee.

"How goes the reporting?" Baylon asked.

"Fine, fine." Viskul waved his hand. "The chaps do their best. Tis only a problem when the *dead* slide through and deliver themselves unannounced on the hallowed grounds of the great Meadow Red," he said with a grim smile.

Grem's hand flashed to his dagger and the queen's guard drew swords advancing. The Tanish Pirate replaced his blade and put his hands calmly on the table while Viskul hacked a rheumy laugh and spat something into a handkerchief. He slurped his coffee noisily, and the queen dismissed Mallon and Amalia before the old bugger could violate every rule of common decency.

"Keep yer blade to yerself, dead man. I don't *care* that *you* came through my forest. I *do* care that I suspect you weren't the only ones. And you," he waved at them all, squinting his age-clouded eyes at them. "Worry me much less than those I haven't yet been able to identify. Tell me, Prince Baylon–what do you understand of this alien king's physiology? Does his heart still beat?"

The question caught him off guard. "I … I'm not sure, Master Viskul. Why do you harbor such grave suspicions?"

"We got a lad in the chambers that's special. Swears he can see the whole of the forest from the tops of the firs. Claims he saw a shadow in the night–a figure cloaked in darkness–only nobody else can verify it. Almost 200 are sleeping in the chambers, and there's not been a single corroboration."

"And this boy–do you believe he holds such a vantage?"

"Aye, the lad's mapped the entire forest. Fully accurate. I consulted with the Arborist."

"And what did *that* old coot have to say?" Scrimshaw asked. He'd enjoyed a game of checkers and an apple brandy with the sole inhabitant of the Watchful Woods.

"He claims he never saw anyone pass through, but that he did feel a terrible presence. It lingered there for weeks, he said, and it left him with a chill."

Baylon nodded. There'd been moments in the woods when he thought he'd felt eyes on him, and not those of the seers of Greentower.

"Tis a dark and secretive place, your woods," Baylon said. "But it's still impenetrable by mortal men, Master Viskul. As long as your seers maintain their connection with the forest, Greentower is safe to the south."

"Bah," the old man said. He looked away, studying a spot on the wall. "Speaking of that very topic, are you going south again soon, Master Baylon?"

"As soon as we're outfitted. We mean to make double time, now that we'll have horses again."

Viskul stood. He touched Baylon's shoulder lightly. "Keep a wary eye in the woods, Master Baylon. I felt it, too–on the day I met with the Arborist. M' Lady." He bowed to the queen before taking his leave.

"Cheery sort, eh?" Grem said.

"He's very protective of the kingdom," Emaline said. "He's served three Fielding kings in his time. He may not be the most politic of generals, but he looks after the seers well, and cares deeply about Greentower."

They finished their breakfast, Baylon's company retreating to the stables to check the status of their mounts. Baylon lingered with his mother at the balcony of the high tower.

"You will do great things, Baylon." She took his hand in hers and rubbed his arm. "You wouldn't have been returned to us if it wasn't so."

Baylon smiled. "Thank you, Mother. I left you years ago on an errand of peace, and now I'm returned to you on the eve of war. Those circumstances sadden me, but I'm happy to be here with you now. I'm happy, in this moment, in this place, to stand in the halls of my youth with my mother."

"Me too, Baylon. Me too."

They were dead, all of them, and once the shock of it left him, Baylon felt a deep and resolute sadness for his fallen companions. Two stable boys had also been killed, and it appeared Grem had likely wounded one of their attackers. A trail of tacky blood–thick in the stable, then petering out into nothing in the lane behind the building–covered the stone floor.

"You must ride, Master Baylon," Killney Scarton said. "Take two of the mounts and make straight away for the Arborist's cottage."

"I have to see my father, Hai Scarton. Is he returned yet from his errands in the south?"

"There's no time for that. Your return to Greentower has made someone very angry. Very angry. And, it appears, very nervous. It's not safe here for you. Here"–pressing his sword into Baylon's hand–"tis handsome iron. A Fielding blade. There are provisions enough for your journey. These men"–he nodded at the slain of Harrow Colony–"will they rise again?"

Baylon shook his head as Scarton shrugged out of his coat. He handed it to the young prince. "You weren't expected here, Master Baylon, but you did your job well. The Ice Barons know what's coming, and that's enough. Now go. Return to your people and strangle the brutes at the Reach."

"Thank you, Hai Scarton. See to it that these men are given a respectable burial."

The guard nodded. He shook the prince's hand and, trailing a second pack horse on a long lead, Baylon set out for the castle gates. He felt exposed in the streets of the city that had once been his home, waiting for an assassin's arrow at every cobbled turn.

Scarton had sent word to the guard. They cracked open a merchant's gate, and Baylon fired out into Meadow Red at a full gallop. He spared a single glance over his shoulder at the great fortress of Greentower before the Watchful Woods swallowed him.

# Daniel Powell

Night falls quickly in the winter, but Baylon Fielding had only been in the woods an hour before lighting a torch. He wouldn't reach the Arborist until the first hours of the new morning, even if he pushed his horses to its limits, so he decided to go easy on the animals.

A unity of snow-covered greenery–firs and pines and the occasional bramble–pushed in from every side. It had been frightening when traveling with companions. On his own, the place terrified.

He snacked on flatbread and pickled fish, riding with his left hand on the sword Scarton had given him.

After many hours on the path, the forest parted and Baylon found himself in a snow-covered meadow. The yellow moon, round and full, shone brightly on a robed figure awaiting him. Baylon approached the man warily.

"Whatever magic brought you back from the grave *can* be undone."

Baylon shivered. He knew that voice, and his suspicion was confirmed when Barkwill removed his hood. A thin rivulet of blood escaped his grim smile, and he dabbed at it with a handkerchief.

"Looks like Grem took a bite out of you," Baylon said. "I'm glad he did. I've always suspected your false loyalties, priest. Step aside, and let me pass."

"Loyalties?" Barkwill laughed. "*Loyalties*? This from the leader of an army of dead men? From a boy, now fleeing the ancestral halls of his youth? Spare me your lectures, Baylon Fielding. I value expediency over loyalty, and I've made *my* choice." He extended his hand. In it was a tiny porcelain box. "Dismount, Baylon. Come. Let me show you the future, if you're bright enough to claim it."

Baylon did, drawing his sword.

"Ah, ah, ah." Barkwill waved his finger. He parted his robes showing Baylon saw the mess that was his stomach. "You can't kill me, boy, I'm already dead. Just like you. It would take a live man–a man with the *vital elements*–to send me to my final rest."

"What's in the box?" Baylon kept the sword at the ready.

"Xerick Khan's reach is long. So … very … *long*, my boy. It stretches to every corner of the five continents. It stretches to the heavens. Khan is coming, Baylon. He is coming, and he means to rule the five continents. You'd do well to join him."

"What *is* it?"

Barkwill opened the box. It was filled with black powder–granules that vibrated with a peculiar energy. The priest dipped the tip of his pinky into the granules; he touched them to his tongue.

For an instant, shadow obscured the man. When it lifted, he stood larger–more visceral somehow. The whites of his eyes glowed in the night. His smile stretched wider.

"Ahhh," he growled. "The power of the ancients. Here, boy. Partake."

Baylon let the sword slip from his grasp.

The powder spoke to him, and he went to it.

"Kahn understands the power of the ancients. Join him," Barkwill whispered. "Join *us*! We will rule the five continents. We will remake the world in our image."

Baylon couldn't control himself; he extended his hand.

"There." Barkwill hissed, "Yes, Baylon. *Yes!* Take it … you'll feel a power unlike anything you've ever known."

Baylon's index finger hovered over the porcelain box. The granules vibrated and hummed. It would be so simple–*so* simple. And he *wanted* to. He was curious–overcome with an insatiable desire flooding through every part of him.

Baylon blinked and there, in that instant of darkness, he saw *them*. His father and mother, slaughtered in the Hall of the Dozens, the statues of his ancestors reduced to rubble. He saw his brothers and sister, executed–their bodies dangling from the gates of a smoldering Greentower. He saw ships crashing on the shores of the Aisle of Spouting Horns, droves of angry Kotharks storming Meadow Red from the north and the south.

And even as he swatted the powder from the dark priest's hand, he felt the blade sliding through his ribs. It bit into him, snatching his breath, and he fell there in the meadow, very near where a dark smudge of celestial powder now stained the snow.

"Fool," Barkwill spat. Stony hatred resonating. "You are finished, Baylon Fielding. There will be no second rising. And there will only be blood and pain for the people of the Brittle Continent–for your family and all you hold dear. You could have spared them, you *fool!*"

Baylon gasped. He touched his chest, his hand coming away covered in tepid blood.

"You … chose …" Baylon panted, fumbling for his dagger, "the …"

Barkwill sneered at him. He leaned in close, his ear mere inches from the dying boy's mouth.

"I chose what, Baylon? Please–enlighten me."

"... the ... wrong ... side," he gasped, driving the blade into the priest's ear. Blood spurted in thick gouts, the traitor dead—dead! for a second, and final, time–before his body hit the snow.

Baylon pushed the body aside. He stared up at the moon, his hand once again finding the gusher of blood at his chest.

Only this time, when his hand came away, it *steamed* mightily. A smile lit the prince's features, and he thought of Holder Brim. Baylon had done it, and in the simple act of sacrifice in the name of his family, he understood how the men of Harrow Colony could reclaim the vital elements.

"*Love*," he said on his last breath, and then the darkness took him.

Master Viskul's seers slept in their chambers, searching. The trees swayed in the frigid wind, the seers peering through swaying branches and out into the stark meadow, but there was no trace of the half-risen prince.

Dark clouds covered the moon; they opened in the night, and the snow erased any trace of the dead men in the meadow. Beyond the woods, an anxious kingdom slept, the pall of nameless dangers and harsh days ahead forming dreams into nightmares.

And a continent to the south, fully half a world distant, the bows of a thousand warships touched open water.

Daniel teaches a variety of writing classes at Florida State College at Jacksonville. He has published numerous short stories and critical essays in journals, anthologies, and magazines, and his most recently released novel is the horror thriller Cold on the Mountain. He is working on his doctoral degree in the Texts and Technology program at the University of Central Florida in Orlando.

Daniel enjoys fishing the tidal creeks of Duval County and jogging the haunted shell mounds of the Timucuan Preserve. He shares a home near Florida's Intracoastal Waterway with his wife, Jeanne, his daughter, Lyla, and his son, Luke.

# The Barred Gate

Clint Spivey

The Cathedral belched the priest from its creaking iron hatch.

"Stay back!"

Eleven-year-old Ivan watched from a group of a dozen men with trembling hands as the head priest, the man who led their order for so many years, spat blood. Weeping blisters gleamed in the weak twilight of dawn, pocking his parchment thin flesh.

"Let none doubt what truly lies behind these walls." The priest motioned to the massive iron building towering over the pines beside it. "My seared skin reveals our ancestor's folly. Lust not after the convenience this power once brought. It serves man no more. Only death awaits those who venture within."

Rising on shaking legs, the priest returned to the doorway of the great, arching structure.

"I join those who've gone before me. My bones beside their own in mute warning to any who disregard the teachings of The Barred Gate."

No one spoke as he shut himself behind the creaking iron door.

As the men chained and anointed the once more sealed portal, the power of that day was not lost upon young Ivan.

Georgi slapped at the furious black cloud engulfing his face. Barely the second week of spring and the beasts swarmed. The Cathedral, visible a kilometer away in an impossible angle, sprang from the trees crowding its very edge. Forty years had passed since anyone last entered the arched structure, three hundred meters in length and sealed within it the folly of a bygone age.

"It's something, isn't it?" a man said, approaching from behind.

"Yes." Georgi remained bent gathering mushrooms. The same

infuriating pests savaging Georgi seemed uninterested in the newcomer.

"Such mysteries left behind. We can puzzle over the ancestor's surplus trinkets for years and barely discern their use. How much longer to understand what rests within that?" He gestured to The Cathedral.

"It holds death, nothing more. The Barred Gate teaches this."

"Tell me, does your religion forbid even questioning the nature of such works?"

Georgi rose to face the visitor. A rough, brown robe trailed from beneath the man's leather jacket. Heavy boots peeked from the long robe's tails.

"What brings you here?" Georgi asked, his own white garments dirty, even to the red trimmed hem.

"When called, one comes." He looked from the horizon to Georgi. "Those pests are a nightmare. Here." He fished around in his pocket and produced a thin band, a piece of ancestor surplus emitting a strong scent. "Wear this strap like a necklace. It will keep them at bay."

Ivan plugged away at his portable game with knitted brows. Georgi swept the wooden floor, avoiding the priest's legs, resting upon a stool. He swept around the unmoving head priest until there was nothing else but to push the broom as close as possible to try and clear the crumbs and dust.

The priest didn't budge, but kept at the beeping surplus game. Spare batteries rested on the table in charging trays, tethered by a thin cable running through the window to the bank of sun panels on the roof. Similar panels, scrounged from ancestor wrecks, tiled every village rooftop visible through the window.

"There was a preacher in the village today," Georgi said.

"Hmm." Ivan didn't look up from his game.

"He spoke of The Cathedral. Of entering it."

"It happens."

"He spoke of enough power within to heat everyone's water daily while providing heat in winter and cool air in summer."

"And you believe such nonsense?"

"The others did. The villagers listening to him, I mean."

"How many were there?"

"About fifteen or twenty."

"And did you answer his lies with the truth of that place? Did you warn the people who might enter against releasing hell's invisible flame?"

The boy looked down. "No. I just listened."

Ivan set down his game. "Do you doubt the danger within that place?"

Georgi knew well the story that followed. Of The Cathedral's consuming fury. The way it seared flesh with neither light nor heat, devouring a man in mere hours.

Except he'd never seen it happen. Not once. Georgi had only the word of a fat, lazy priest.

The pews of their tiny chapel lay near empty. Ivan could count on one hand how many sat in attendance. He'd spent nearly twenty minutes preparing his sermon, and only a few old men and women were there.

"We make ready to renew the seals of that foul place," Ivan said from the pulpit. "The ceremony, an ancient one, is no less important today than when The Cathedral was sealed long ago. I hope you'll tell your families and friends, who it saddens me are not here this evening, to join us for this important event."

The congregation dwindled by the week. Georgi, Ivan's only acolyte, stood bored in the back while the elderly flock filed out.

"We must begin visitation," Ivan said to Georgi, when they were alone. "To remind them of our order. We must see the flock replenished."

He'd been a good shepherd, Ivan told himself. Many of the village youth departed for the city, where ancestor surplus abounded, and even periodic electricity could be found. Such flight was normal. Older parishioners, once his source of congregation, had always made up for their children's departure.

But as other deacons and brothers died, few took their place, until only Ivan and Georgi remained stewards of The Barred Gate.

"They go to see the preacher. We can visit them there."

Ivan rubbed his temples. "Do you proselytize in his name? Don't forget who took you in when you were naked and starving in the woods."

"I forget nothing." The boy's tone was sharp. "But if you ask me which doctrine to follow; ours with dwindling followers, or the one with actual converts, I think the choice is clear."

Ivan readied further rebuff but paused, his shoulders slumping. "I suppose we should go."

"See the Angel of Light spreading her wings?" The preacher asked, raising his hands to the red symbol on a yellow field behind him. A smaller such icon hung from his neck. "She welcomes us with her light. Cradles us beneath her wings. We need only put aside fear."

Ivan had to admit, it did resemble an angel. Radiating out from a central circle, the trio of triangular shapes flared out at the circle's ten, two, and six o'clock positions. If the pair on top were wings, the third at the bottom resembled flowing robes.

Revival was in the air. Faces beamed at the preacher's words, delivered with a hopeful sincerity that touched even Ivan.

But The Barred Gate did not dispense hope, false or otherwise. Their message was caution: warning against the idleness of their ancestors that brought about the destruction housed within The Cathedral. Watching the almost joyous proceedings around him, replete with refreshments and a crackling bonfire, Ivan saw to which message the people flocked.

"Our pilgrimage begins soon. We will tear down the walls encircling The Cathedral, and bask in The Angel's warming glow."

What was once blasphemy, now drew cheers. The order took Ivan in, just another orphan boy, and showed kindness where others had not. Accepting their bizarre beliefs regarding the mountainous iron building rising from the trees had seemed a small price in exchange for clean clothes, food, and a bed. That day, forty years past, watching the priest's dying exit, Ivan saw the truth of their words.

The village provided comfort enough that the memory of the horrid death had rarely tainted Ivan's daily indulgences. A few tired, yearly processions to bless the sealed portal, earned him sufficient tithe to live in comfort.

But around this preacher were many young faces Ivan didn't recognize.

Had he truly wasted so many years?

Listening to the preacher amid his swelling congregation, Ivan saw the future. The Barred Gate, the order that for 200 years kept watch over the peril within The Cathedral, would die. It's epitaph bearing Ivan's name.

Ivan dragged a wooden chest from beneath his bed.

"Just a foolish old man," the priest said, unlatching the case. "Is that what you think?"

Georgi screwed up his courage. "The preacher's growing throng is proof enough. You admonish me to preach to them, yet you teach me little yourself. How am I to be earnest when you are not? It is a poor schoolmaster whose own passion fades."

"You may be many things, boy, but you are no coward." Ivan raised the lid. "Nor a fool. Learn what that place holds."

The cloth bound books within held photos. The colors faded but retaining clarity enough to reveal the old world: full of the garments and trinkets their vanished ancestors took for granted. There were people costumed in shiny suits of white or yellow, sealing their wearers down to heavy gloves, their eyes hidden beneath goggles and mouths behind filters that hung past their chins.

"What is this?" Georgi asked.

"The end of that place." Ivan turned a page. There were more photos. Men. And women. Their bare skin marked by burns. Each pitiful victim rested in what was clearly some healing house bed, their expressions devoid of any hope.

"These were the first," Ivan said. "On the day the fire emerged from one of their impossible machines. These were the ones who came to try and solve whatever problem they unleashed that day. In two days' time, those men were reduced"–he flipped a page–"to that." He tapped a thick finger to the shredded victims surrounded by the masked others. "There's more."

There was no lack of horror in that trunk. Most were photos of adults, all wearing the same seared skin. Others, of children, dead and alive bearing deformities such as Georgi had not witnessed in nightmares.

Beastly, twisted things that were only too recognizable as his own species.

"That is the power of that place," the priest said. "That is what the invisible fire does to those who enter."

"Why build such machines?"

Ivan shook his head. "The preacher is right about the place. It once flung power beyond the horizon. It fed their homes in the thousands. It was tamed, that fire. Forced to warm them in winter and warped through their artifice to cool the summer.

"But it was not docile. When it escaped, it tore through these men with a vengeance that sloughed the skin from them. And it remains, cursing that place with its power. Content within The Cathedral, but only too eager to visit its pain upon any who enter."

Georgi closed the book. "Why not show the villagers? With such proof, you could counter the preacher's words."

Ivan shook his head. "Those people no longer care for our truth. They want what he preaches. Easy, abundant power. Enough to warm their homes during the snows. Extra to warm their water and their stew. The life of ease that our ancestors squandered."

"He seeks to lead them inside. They'll be killed."

"In ways more painful than you can imagine, boy. No. They would wave away these images. But there is one thing that even the preacher and his throngs wouldn't be able to ignore.

Georgi pulled at an item on the bottom. A sealed, plastic pouch with square lumps within.

"What's this?" Georgi held up the sealed package.

"Stop pestering me, boy. It's just some relic surplus for further sealing The Cathedral. Your duty is to search out some of these truths yourself. How else will you learn when I'm gone?" Ivan left the room.

A small booklet was clipped to the package's side. Chastened, Georgi read it.

The bonfire lit the village center with a harsh glow, setting shadows to dance about a wooden stage. Ivan approached the group of a hundred or so people without speaking.

The crackling flames offered little competition to the preacher's burning fervor. "When we renew the power within The Cathedral, we need not fear winter's wrath. But will instead greet it as our ancestors did, as simply another turn of our planet as it chases its course about the sun. For our baths will steam amidst nights lit once more beyond mere flame."

The crowd muttered their praise. Their reverence on display in the casual acceptance of his words that demanded no shouting. Ivan waited for a brief pause to speak.

"Have you known anything to be so simple?" he said, his own barrel chest propelling his voice across the crowd. A hundred gazes fell upon him as he approached the dais where the preacher stood.

"Do you think The Barred Gate preaches our message to keep people in hunger and cold? Do you think I, of all people, would not enjoy steaming baths and lighted houses while the snow piles in banks outside my home? Do I preach caution because I prefer hardship?" He reached the dais and stopped, a single foot upon the steps. "I ask you, preacher. If you be a fair judge of men, do you suspect lies from me?"

The preacher watched Ivan for several heartbeats before speaking. His voice was not unkind. "I believe, friend, that you have been led astray. For the Angel of Light"–he gestured to the radiating icon behind him–"has brought me here to reclaim that power. Perhaps it was once deadly to enter The Cathedral, but over two hundred winters have passed since the old world fell. Surely whatever death resided within lingers no more."

"Eight hundred winters could pass and the unseen fire would be no less diminished than the day it spilled from our ancestors' great chamber. But I will no longer ask those here to put faith in my words alone. I will instead demonstrate the peril that entry entails."

The preacher cocked his head. "Good priest. How do you intend to demonstrate this if The Cathedral is yet sealed? We have not begun our pilgrimage to crack its mighty shell." The preacher's gaze narrowed. "Unless there is yet some truth you have withheld from those around us." He gestured to the crowd.

Ivan climbed the dais and gazed out at the crowd.

"There is, I admit, knowledge that I and the others before me have kept hidden."

"You have already entered it, haven't you?" the preacher asked.

"No. And this is the truth. For all who enter suffer and perish in a matter of hours. But I have witnessed one enter. And the effect it had upon him."

"You offer little more than a sermon."

Ivan looked at the man beside him. "If only a sermon would suffice. I have grown soft in my years. I see now, that my penance for such sloth requires the ultimate sacrifice. My people"–he turned to the crowd–"I will show you what lies within that place. I will enter The Cathedral. And when I emerge, sickened and burned, and when you see my cursed body, then, will you believe."

The preacher watched Ivan without speaking. His usual confidence diluted as he thought on the older man's words.

"This hour tomorrow," Ivan said. "I shall enter. I ask only that all who seek entrance, wait for dawn to witness my emergence."

"I shall accompany him!" the preacher said. "If the way inside has been revealed, then I, too, shall enter. To show you"–he gestured to Ivan–"and everyone that we need not fear." His smile was beset with the worry that accompanies prophecy unfolding in a manner unforeseen.

"Very well," Ivan said. "Since I doubt you will be dissuaded, we enter together. I bid you, good preacher, settle any Earthly affairs you might have. For the sunrise we witness upon leaving that place, will be our last."

The crowd was quiet now. For few could doubt the sincerity bleeding into Ivan's words. He departed the dais amidst a silent crowd.

The preacher waved away the proffered lantern. "The light of creation within is all the light I require." The two sat at Ivan's table the following evening while Georgi readied food.

Ivan pushed the lantern toward the man again. "Then carry it for me. My lack of faith blinds me to that which guides you."

The preacher squinted before accepting the lantern. "Very well."

Georgi placed a plate of food before each man.

Ivan pushed his plate away. "That place wreaks havoc upon ones bowels. I wish to enter on as light a stomach as possible."

"You're skipping a meal?" Georgi asked, incredulous. "If you seek to demonstrate your resolve even to me, I assure you, a plate of potatoes and eggs will not aid that."

"Have you said your farewells?" Ivan asked the preacher.

"I spoke with the faithful. They await my return."

Ivan shook his head. "This is nothing to be taken lightly. Accept that, with the slightest of possibilities, this trip is as perilous as I claim. Ought you not to speak to those you care about with an earnest heart?"

"My faith will carry me through."

"I will say no more, then. But know that what you carry out of that place will deal death to those you come into contact with."

"Shall we depart?" the preacher asked.

Ivan turned to Georgi. "I know the doubts you harbor. After this day, they will trouble you no more. You will find all of the texts you require to carry on in my stead once I am gone. Everything is in my bedchambers, which, when I depart, will be your bedchambers. I have trust in you to assume my responsibilities."

"And if he is correct?" Georgi asked. "And the place is safe?"

"Then you will see me tomorrow, and I expect tea upon my return."

Georgi stood at the fore of the crowd jostling to see the two men enter the Cathedral. Nearly the entire village gathered in two distinct groups, one much larger than the other.

"This will be our final autumn of hardship," the preacher said. "You will feast in warmth beside smiling children before the first snows fall."

"I hope you remember that I promise nothing so sweet," Ivan said. "Yet I fear I will be the more reviled when you see the truth seared into my flesh. For hopes dashed are not as suspect as truth revealed. Perhaps it is a blessing that I will not long live with your judgment."

And so they entered, disappearing through the slab of a door into the depths. Georgi was the last to see both men disappear into the darkness. Before sealing the door, he risked a look after them, and saw only black.

## The Barred Gate

"By heaven," the preacher said.

"Yes," Ivan held his lantern high, it's feeble light lost in the cavernous space. An eternity of darkness rose to heights that rivaled where stars dwell. Two tiny islands of light banishing the dusty gloom were all the men had to guide them. Ivan stepped forward.

The ruined building emerged before them, hinting at its shape until their light struck its ruined walls.

"My flock wondered of the ancient's prowess," the preacher said. "They will marvel at this."

Ivan squinted in the lamplight at his map. "This way."

The preacher kicked about the rubble. "What great calamity befell them? What error, so common of the ancients, led this place to fall?"

"As with all of their faults, it was arrogance. The pride that arose from a life of comfort. They harnessed such power, and in the end they treated it as a toy."

"Where they squandered, we will appreciate. Three lifetimes of nature's harsh tutelage has readied us as proper stewards."

Ivan's temples throbbed but he remained silent. What now devoured them cared not for sermons.

"The entrance." Ivan pointed.

"I must commend your order," the preacher said at the door. "You maintained accurate records. And look! The Angel's mark." Faded red and yellow markings, matching the preacher's own banner, hid behind thick dust. "How can you deny such images?"

Ivan scrutinized his map. The place was as much maze as mausoleum. Stairs, rooms, hallways branching into piles of debris that arrested their progress; while the preacher saw signs, Ivan fought to keep from getting lost. If not for the certainty that any living thing entering this place soon died, he might have feared the darkness. Instead, he feared only making it his tomb.

"This way," he said after finding the path once more. Rusted metal stairs rang their descent as the two delved below ground.

"The Angel's light fills me," The preacher said, ecstasy in his voice. "Do you not feel it, priest?"

"I do. Though it does not fill, but consume."

"You err, good priest. It is but the shock of souls lain dormant for so long. As our eyes, unaccustomed to the dawn snap shut at its brilliance. So do our spirits tremble to feel the Angel filling them once more."

Gravel crunched beneath Ivan's feet. "This is the basement," he said. "We have arrived."

The sketch on Ivan's map was crude; a pencil shaded thing that, despite its rushed appearance was accurate. The lump, or "foot", as labeled on the weathered parchment, stood before them.

"There," Ivan said. "That is the source of their power." Ivan's head spun. Whatever burned in that place was at its strongest in the basement. The preacher, by contrast spoke with a zeal rivaling his fiery sermons.

"Yes. I feel it. The power of creation. Harnessed by our ancestors. Bent to serve by their prowess. And by the Angel's guidance, we've arrived from bleary waking dream, through hardships and winter snows, to this." He knelt beside the man-sized lump of misshapen metal at the source of this corruption, and threw up, retching his previous meal upon the floor with violence.

"Perhaps such power overwhelms my earthly constitution." Doubt crept behind his words. "I must sit down."

"Not here," Ivan said. "If you choose, you can return with the heartiest of your flock and bring forth this relic. For now, let us depart before our lanterns fail."

"You speak prudence. Let us go."

The preacher was quieter on their return, stopping only to look and mumble at each yellow and red sign upon the walls. Ivan, fighting his own nausea, focused on his map.

"We can rest now," Ivan said once they had cleared the structure. "I wouldn't have thought this darkness a thing of respite. But after that place, this cavern is welcome."

The preacher sat beside him. "Do you know why I came?"

"Your dream," Ivan said. "The same to which all cling. A return to our ancestors' level of learning. It's nothing to be ashamed of."

"I had a child once," his voice quiet. "A girl. Born in winter, against all wisdom. But such accidents happen when two people are in love, as her mother and I were. In the end, when she came early, we fought to warm her in our tiny oven, as a shepherd does with a lamb." He sifted the dirt through his fingers. "She died within hours, lying shrouded in our home until spring. We buried her in the thawed ground.

"Our ancestors were untroubled by such events. Their numbers swelled the Earth, such was their mastery of the world. I sought only to prevent any other family from nature's cruel fortune."

Ivan was silent. His head swam in the glow of their lanterns.

"We will die," the preacher said. "Just as you predicted."

"I did nothing with a vengeful heart. I've lived too slothful a life, shirked my duties until the people regarded my warning as those of a man watching his full larder in threat of emptying." Ivan kicked at the broken earth beneath them. "Your hope was equal to my failure."

"And here we now sit. I can feel it consuming me from within, as I'm sure you can. Is your young acolyte prepared to accept your responsibilities?"

Ivan laughed, the sound vanishing into the darkness. "Before, or after he welcomes my absence?"

The iron door shrieked upon its hinges, signaling their exit into the morning twilight.

"We return," the preacher said.

Hope glistened in a hundred eyes.

"What did you see?"

"When can we heat our homes?"

The preacher raised his arms as if to embrace his flock. "I have seen the might and power of the Angel within. It glows with a radiance that touches me even now." Gasps of joy erupted from the faithful.

"But such is not yet for us." The chain bearing his icon snapped as he flung it from his neck to the ground. "It was no Angel that dwelled within. Only burning death as your priest claimed.

Ivan looked at the man beside him.

The preacher continued, "This power burns yet unchained. To try and bind it once more, as our ancestors did, invites darkness." He held up his blistered arms. "It would invite your deaths." He looked to Ivan. "As it invited ours."

Disappointment washed over the preacher's followers like a polluted tide. Ivan smiled.

"Good people," Ivan said. "Your preacher is mistaken. The light within has filled us with its poison. As vessels, we've leeched away its corruption. The two of us driving it from that holy place so that it is safe.

Do you hear? It is made safe!"

"What? How can you–"

Ivan clapped a hand to the preacher's shoulder. "It is the Angel's enigma to pull doubt from one while another takes it up. I thank you, preacher, for you have shown me my error."

Ivan turned to the crowd. "Fetch your lanterns, and candles to light the darkness. Rations. Water. For the return inside will require long hours of toil to reheat our homes and relight our streets.

"Bring your tools. Your strong boys to labor within and your dutiful girls to aid them. You have endured your final perilous winter. This season, your children will bathe in steaming water during nights lit bright with our ancestor's secrets. Now, go! We enter before the sun strikes noon."

The people cheered. Laughed. Ran for their supplies.

"You promised them light," Ivan said. "I will bring it to them."

"You doom them," the preacher said as his congregation fled, singing and praising. "How can you deny that which eats away our very flesh as we yet stand?"

Georgi remained, removed by several paces.

"I deny nothing. I will give the people the miracle they crave. And when the doubters in my flock see their faith rewarded, The Barred Gate will thrive unchallenged for a century." He turned to Georgi. "One dead priest, fat and despised, won't ensure our order. But a hundred? Women, children, innocents all? That is Godly wrath the likes of which will be recounted for generations. Be thankful, boy. I've handed you an enviable position."

Georgi's clenched fists trembled. "Even at your end, you are at your most vile."

Ivan, on unsteady legs, turned to join the departing villagers.

"I must thank you, preacher," he called back from the trees. "You made this possible."

"You must warn them," the preacher said to Georgi. "If that which poisons me, spreads, I will doom them myself."

"Perhaps I can do more than that," the boy said before sprinting away.

# The Barred Gate

There was no empty ritual for the devices. Just a few, surprisingly simple steps. The soft blocks attached to the rusted metal with little effort, like potter's clay. He arranged them upon the walls on both sides just outside the entrance before piercing them with the metal tipped chords with which the guide instructed. The last step was to operate the device by remote. A small thing of ancient surplus with smooth, machined edges and a display that lit with their artifice. Two batteries, pilfered from Ivan's portable game, snapped into place. A red light atop the device glowed in answer.

"This will seal it? You are certain?" the preacher asked.

"I'm certain of nothing. The instructions carried warnings. It would be best to stay back."

The preacher shook his head. "If we can't seal this portal, many will die today besides Ivan and me."

Voices arose from the trees.

"Go! Hide from sight but not my voice. Listen for the sign to activate your device."

"How will I know your sign?"

"If I retain any talent for swaying men's reason, you will know when to act."

Georgi nodded before running toward the trees.

"Ah, Preacher," Ivan said as his procession entered the clearing before the gate. "Will you reconsider?"

The preacher rushed forward to the clearing's edge, halting the crowd as far as he could from the portal.

"Stop, if you value your lives. For the Angel has revealed truth to me this day. He will smite those who disregard his warnings."

"Join us, preacher. Join us in bringing comfort and security to them and their little ones." Ivan gestured to the men, women, and smiling children at his back. Women praised the Angel's light while rocking their young too small to walk. Men pumped fists and exhorted the priest at their head.

Ivan stepped forward. "Why do you doubt the very Angel that called you?"

The preacher matched Ivan's steps, grateful the crowd remained unmoved at the clearing's edge. "I saw what you saw. And though I know you as false, I seek not your conversion." The preacher looked to the crowd. "He leads you astray. For a terrible blow will strike if you proceed for that door." A rock sailed past his head. Jeers followed in its wake.

Ivan clapped a massive hand on the preacher's shoulder. "It is not wise to challenge the heavens," he said. "Our ancestors knew this in their old religion. You ought not do so now." Vitriol, unseen to the crowd, dripped from Ivan's smile. The preacher squirmed from Ivan's mighty grasp and ran towards the door.

"Behold, the power you would disregard!" he said, hands raised in the air.

Nothing happened.

Georgi clutched the surplus device in trembling hands. Ivan followed the preacher toward the gate. The preacher raised his hands, and while the their words were barely audible, he gathered this was the sign. He closed his eyes and pressed the switch. A simple click answered.

Deep, metal booms pierced the forest hush from the crowd's thrown stones bouncing at The Cathedral's metal sides. Georgi pressed the switch, again and again, without response.

It couldn't be. Georgi fought the urge to fling the worthless device, but instead inspected it. He turned a clicking knob several times but there was nothing from the device.

The crowd stirred. Lone men moved with purpose toward the preacher who called upon thunder from above to halt their blasphemies.

"Ancestor … shit," Georgi said, and clicked the knob another turn. A green light replaced the red atop the device. *Green. Did that mean?* He looked up and pressed the button once more.

The world lurched. Georgi thought himself punched by some unseen assailant, so fast was he thrown to the ground. The world vanished in a wave of dust. Dulled screams emerged from the haze and met his ringing ears. Georgi stood, and, tucking away the device in a pocket, stumbled to the gate.

Hell lay before him. Men and women writhed upon the ground. Their noses and ears seeped blood. From the halest man to the tiniest child, none were spared. They screamed and shuddered on the ground before him. But all moved.

He turned toward the gate. By heaven, what had he unleashed? Of the preacher, Ivan, indeed the gate, and the few men who'd approached it, nothing remained. A great hole rent the earth where the gate once pierced the structure. Half buried in a pile of stone and twisted steel, a crater gaped in a semicircle from beneath the arching Cathedral.

The people rose. In the moment before the panic of their bleeding children overtook them, they saw Georgi. The red trim of his Barred Gate raiment shining through the smoking ruin. Where blood coursed from their orifices, he stood with a light coating of dust. And they fled.

"See now!" Georgi yelled, his voice halting their flight. "The door remains closed. Those who would enter, risk such fury."

He felt little better than his old master, who'd feasted upon their tithed foods while their stomachs rumbled. He'd brought more suffering upon them than Ivan ever had. And yet, they looked upon him with a fear and reverence that even the preacher had never drawn forth.

Perhaps Georgi understood more of the two men than he realized. He followed the throng to the village, offering succor and aid where he could; for there were many injured, and they wept and screamed as they returned to their homes.

And their story lasted for generations: of the thunder that fell that day, and sealed The Cathedral once more.

Clint Spivey spent eight years working as a meteorologist, first in Europe, then Asia. After finishing grad school, he now teaches English as a foreign language at a university in Tokyo. He now finds himself navigating the academic waters of publish-or-perish. While searching for some unexplored aspect of his field in which to add to the knowledge base, he wishes his few speculative fiction sales were appropriate for bolstering his professional resume. The same for his meager TESOL publications when submitting cover letters to speculative fiction markets. His fiction has appeared most recently in Fantasy Scroll Mag, SQ Mag, and Perihelion.

# Book of Being

Lee Clark Zumpe

*Beneath the gray sky ablaze with pitch,*
*Upon the fields sodden by the blood of soldiers*
*Four Dassmen met the Armies of Sisneunamah.*

*The Four Dark Keeps shall be silent evermore*
*Nevermore shall blades fall over the Namolah Blood Altar,*
*And by Sword and by Spell shall Sisneunamah be conquered.*

## I

Dawn drew old Sanggruth the Glum out of his motley little tent; a smelly, ragged canopy cut from the hide of a wild zurk long ago. Alongside dozens of similar tents, Sanggruth's sat neatly pitched upon a grassy rise just outside the walls of Harchil.

Sanggruth the Glum drew the flap down and stepped out onto the dew-damp grass. He regarded the sky, eyeing it with a trace of reverence. He ran a knotted finger over dry lips, pulled the cloak hood over his head, and set out toward the city.

With a measured gait–checked by a wound to his leg scored many years ago–he trod the velvety sod and approached the White Gate. Before the massive door Sanggruth stood silently, granting the guardians of the watchtowers ample time to be dazzled by the utter resplendence of his ceremonial garb.

Down upon him they gazed from their stations, studying him wordlessly. His purple robe with golden emblems billowed in the gentle breeze, and the fringed ends of the red sash curled and fluttered. Following this brief inspection, the portcullis and gate groaned open to admit him.

As he passed between the twin watchtowers into the short tunnel-vault, something assaulted his senses. He staggered, recognizing a presence he had not anticipated. Sensing something deep-rooted and overwhelming, he acknowledged a kind of force rarely experienced. Steadying himself, he set onward about his business though the heat, the stench, and the tension of malevolence hung thick in the air.

It could not be ignored.

Beyond the White Gate, within the perimeter of insurmountable bulwarks, Sanggruth beheld once more the sprawling tract of land dubbed the Sacred Valley. The outer curtain enclosed a terrific expanse of verdant land garnished by a sizable forest and an immense lake. To the west, flourishing crops grew in terraced fields–enough food to nourish the populace of the city.

In the center of it all crouched the glorious borough, its gleaming golden spires already sparkling in the rays of ancient Thulmuchi. And there, on the meandering, red-clay road over the rolling knolls toward Harchil, Sanggruth gazed upon representatives from all the far-flung provinces. He, an accomplished Dassman and Elder to the Arts, smiled as he waded into to the throngs who had come to take part in this Day of Repentance.

Small wooden stalls of crude construction lined the Merry Path. These booths brimmed with flowery garments aglow in exotic colors, adorned with strange bowls and painted urns from the distant and troubled Middle Realms. Like wolves, the shop-keeps howled for passersby to inspect their goods. The road crept with sluggish progress as celebrants milled about dreamily. Some of the more brilliant standards caught Sanggruth's eye as he moved along. He found the black and red symbols of the House Til'Adia, poised atop the bannerwands of a company of pilgrims, particularly striking.

As he proceeded, the peasants shouted and bickered, and merchants preached yarns–which were themselves half the worth of their ware. Sanggruth, increasingly aware of the lurking presence behind the scenes, came to conclude its probable origins; and, he knew he would be derelict in his duties if he did not make an effort to confirm his fears.

Yet, the old Dassman also knew what he sought would not be found amid the hordes of peddlers which ran the length of the Merry Path, but within the outer fringes of the city-proper. Only in such environs could the spawn of the High Witch of the Ampehr Mires scavenge for relics in near anonymity.

## II

At mid-day, he came upon the Avenue of Magicians. The heat dampened his skin with sweat, and he found himself short of breath. Sanggruth, a young man no more, felt the onset of exhaustion and knew he must pace himself. More than ever, he found his staff of gnarled oak indispensable, for without its support he could not have made the trek across the valley to this unusual marketplace. Rather irked by his deteriorating health, he cursed his age–and time itself.

Sanggruth immersed himself into a muddle of trinkets, charms, amulets, and yellowed scrolls of scarcely legible cryptic verses. Precious stones were the treasure sold by one; another offered unborn mortal babies extracted from the womb at the first physical sign of pregnancy, and then sheathed in sticky sap. The Temple Sorcerers and High Wizards of the Order Banuki chattered alongside a handful of necromancers and common diviners. Sanggruth glimpsed a smiling, toothless shaman bartering sacks of herbs for a flask of Goolsberry wine, and a red-haired Fire-in-Hand charring segments of dried log to the pleasure of a crowd.

All the magicians in the whole of Mistorel, and from neighboring territories much-influenced by Mistorel's ways, came together under the ancient Covenant of Oulahzu. The Alliance of Adepts embraced them all. The members of this pact convened during the period surrounding the Day of Repentance, a holiday of the realm celebrated but once every fifty years.

On the Day of Repentance, expectation saw each citizen offer up a humble and sincere apology to his gods, not for the sins committed–for sins were dealt with in the afterlife–but for the remorse felt for those things left undone.

This Convergence of Oulahzu happened to be the third and final one to occur during Sanggruth's magically-extended lifespan. Other Dassmen, a fortunate few, lived to see four. Sanggruth could remember nothing of the first such event in which he participated.

Sighting a stall shaded by giant Mithlum leaves, and packed mostly with aged tomes, Sanggruth ventured in for closer inspection. His twisted digits trembled as they fumbled over stacks of texts and mounds of individual and unrelated pieces of parchment. The leathery skin of his own hands closely mirrored the parched and cracked covers of some of the more vintage, arcane works.

One old book caught Sanggruth's eyes. His gnarled hands pawed at its binder, pitch black and dark as the heart of a starless winter night. Finding the tome uncannily captivating, he struggled to keep from being enthralled by the dark magic he suspected lurked within that shadow-wrapped tome.

To the touch, the pages were warm and supple. He found no need to squint his sore and clouded eyes to read the text, for the words leapt from the paper and spoke inside his head. The voice delivering these words came smooth, and sharp, and full of power.

He felt the presence once more touch his soul, burn him. As he lifted his eyes from the tome, the sun seemed to wink. He wondered at that which he held in his grasp, but he knew. He *knew*.

Sanggruth shivered.

The warmth of the day abandoned him as he stood there clutching his find. Covetously gripping the old book close against his chest, an unexpected sense of panic arose from the notion that his discovery might attract the attention of others. He could not allow that to happen, not before a time of thoughtful consideration.

But time he no longer possessed.

Sanggruth staggered into the shadows, allowing the mountains of books to obscure himself from the crowds. Perhaps, he thought, his age and fears and failing powers had rallied together to make him see something that was not there? This thing he held … it could not exist, could it?

Regardless, most certainly it remained a masterpiece of some forgotten age. It was something scribed in blood. He could feel the pulse of conquered souls beating within its pages. Its author remained remote and unknowable, his aura contained within its aging covers but well-concealed behind delicate deceptions. The book refused to reveal to him its source.

But could it truly be what he believed? Could the text in his grasp be *The Namolah Blood Treatise* of Sisneunamah?

Sanggruth toyed with the thought as images of Sisneunamah's army of corpses flooded his mind. If some rogue recovered that occult work from the pits, its bearer could locate the Four Dark Keeps–the Namolah Blood Altar would once more drink of the innocent.

No, it could not be so. His advanced age had him believing in dubious fables. He dared flip further than the first few pages, only to make certain, but even as the words leapt into his mind there came another voice …

"Fair afternoon, good Dassman." An exceptionally tall mystic with a hawkish face approached Sanggruth. He wore a grim countenance and possessed a gaunt figure. His milky eyes studied the Dassman mindfully. There seemed a hint of recognition in his gaze. "Sanggruth the Glum, are you not? This makes four elder Dassmen."

"How many were expected?" he asked with a hint of irritation. His hand hesitantly departed the dark book, and its cover slammed shut sending up a swirl of dust–or was it smoke–into the air. Relinquishing it to a nearby table helped dispel some of his apprehension. Then, recalling the task at hand, Sanggruth's expression dimmed. His eyes could not hold to the man, and his head drooped to stare at the floor. "Is Thoriitch of Nutt to be one?"

"He has already come and gone. They all have, I am sorry to say." Regali's broad hand grasped the Dassman's shoulder, and together they walked out of the stall. "As you know, you are late … the Opening Day has passed. We should be on our way."

The solemnity of their reunion struck Sanggruth as a tragic, unavoidable, finale–one ancient custom had fated. Though he would never admit to it, he often wished the pledge that tied him to Regali left room for camaraderie beyond the ceremonial alliance. Time for such musings had passed, though.

"There is something I should finish, something disturbing I found amongst these old tomes. For a moment, I thought I might have felt–" Sanggruth muttered. The mists which had clouded his mind since walking through the White Gate suddenly dissipated. There was no great evil here; he was simply deluding himself–an old fool looking for a reason to live.

"What were you saying?"

"Nothing. Let us be on our way."

They departed the book dealer's stall, and Sanggruth all but forgot his discovery. For the moment, his decision to pass over the book without further enquiry engendered no trace of remorse. Sorting out such enigmas should be the obligation of younger generations.

Walking farther down the Avenue of Magicians, Sanggruth examined the strange gray garb of the Mesenna'Ala. A relatively new faction of the Alliance of Adepts. Their followers practiced Spiritual Consciousness and, unlike most of their fellow magicians, shunned material possessions. With their heads shaven and adorned by a single red line running around the scalp above the brow, three of them marched by chanting some meditative refrain. Sanggruth loosed a whimsical grunt, doubting they and their pitiful pantheon of one god would accomplish much.

"Do not mock them," cautioned Regali. "I expect that they will do well in the coming epochs."

"Such a preposterous faith," Sanggruth exclaimed bitterly. "You mean to say that it shall outlast the others?"

"No one concept will ever ultimately prevail above all others; but theirs shall be the model for many ages henceforth. This I have been told by keen geomancers and starspellers alike."

Just then, the wails of Newbloods resounded. From a massive canopy of bright yellow tarp, the sound arose, piercing through the clamor of merchants' testimonies and patrons' quarreling. A sound not wholly familiar to most members of the Alliance, since common Magickal Pacts disallow mating.

Sanggruth listened conscientiously. There were large banners boldly displayed around this tent, written in every known language but addressed to only one sect of the Alliance: The signs banned the child-eating Ruthian Conjurers from entering the grounds adjacent the Newblood tent.

"Do you care to see the Newbloods?" he asked Sanggruth.

"No … not this time. I beheld those at the Feast fifty years ago."

"Yes, I was there. Of course, I do not truly remember you. I'm afraid we must part now … I must serve the Line. You shall find what you seek in the adjacent tarpaulin." He motioned toward a small black tent, the entry of which offered no glimpse of its contents. From without, it looked like a bleak, black chunk of eternal night.

Dassman Regali departed Sanggruth's company and entered the Newblood tent. Without moving, the elder Dassman watched through the breach in the fabric as Regali approached a bundle of cushions. Upon these were three infants, unclothed and screaming. Regali knelt down, his robe cascading to the floor, and scooped one of the children into his arms. Holding the child, Regali next approached a figure stationed at the far side of the tent–one Sanggruth knew to be the Nameskeeper. Sanggruth heard Regali take the most sacred vow of the Dassmen and give his foundling a name.

"This child shall be Cullimmanari'Ra-Turen, most Knowledgeable Dassman and Oathson of Regali. From the essence of one, another."

Sanggruth moved on, making his way toward the black tent. He leaned heavily on his staff as he walked. Either fatigue or a wave of nostalgia slowed his progress and caused him to pause occasionally.

During each short respite, he remembered fondly the previous Feast of Masters. Then, he had entered the Newblood tent and selected his own Oathson. There had been instances when he regretted that as an Oathfather he was not permitted to raise his Newblood choice. But, as tradition dictated, he had found a capable set of parents for the child, who accepted the boy as their own. The rudimentary wisdom of a Dassman was present at birth, so the Oathfather had no real duty other than the locating of suitable guardians. The two might never again meet until the Oathson performed his Duty of Thanks by accompanying his elder on the Last Walk.

Inside the black tent, there was but one book. Sanggruth admired it with curiosity. The tome rested upon the crown of a bone-white marble pillar. Many thousands of dry, brownish pages held by exquisite binding, its face a marvelous splendor of finely carved wood. Gleaming golden letters spelled out an unpronounceable title, unknown to even Dassman.

His fingers, less affected by their age, pulsed over the covering. With fervent hands he opened the book, astonished by the brilliant contents. Pictures, vivid with mood and hue, seemed to live and breathe with animation; words and incantations spoke themselves, as though the reader need not even have open eyes to comprehend the text.

Within he perceived tales often spoken of during his days, and figures he knew from life and story. He witnessed his Oathfather and lifelong colleague Thoriitch amongst the throngs of images unveiled and, gradually, his apprehension waned. After all, Sanggruth had lived a long life and now grew weary.

For only an instant his gaze strayed from these pages, to look momentarily over his shoulder in the direction of the door. He was not frightened to find it no longer behind him … nor was he startled the din of outside activities pierced no more this most glorious shrine. All apprehension had been drawn out of his soul as the faces and voices, perfumes and scents waned–and that suffocating dread, which had gripped him earlier, almost completely dulled.

Fleetingly, he thought of his Oathson, Regali, hoping someday the man would join him. How long would it take for fifty more years to pass? As the *Book of Being* drew him within, Sanggruth wondered if time there was even discernible.

Shortly thereafter, the Nameskeeper entered the black tent. Only a handful saw him go in, and fewer still paid attention as he departed moments later, a troubled look upon his face.

With the eventful dawn of the following day, none were available to question why on this particular Convergence of Oulahzu there were fewer Newbloods than ever before.

## III

Regali awoke. He lay beneath heavy fur blankets, his head resting on a plush cushion. The night grew colder than expected, and he was glad to have bartered for a pack of heatstones the previous day. From within his small conical a spiteful wind shrieked along with the stirrings of pilgrims outside.

The night spawned an unexpected storm.

Regali glanced at the Newblood, still slumbering, before tossing aside his coverings and dressing. Though it was still dark, morning could not be far off. He intended to leave just after dawn and make his way back along the old merchant road, searching the farming villages in the Edareauq province for prospective parents.

One regret that weighed heavily on this Dassman's soul was he had not sought to become more familiar with his Oathfather. Sanggruth the Glum would be remembered as one of the most knowledgeable and charitable of all Dassmen, yet Regali knew little more about him than which he had learned from the tales of travelers. Regali believed Sanggruth, too, would have liked a better acquaintance with his Oathson … he believed he read that sentiment in the old Mystic's eyes in the short time they'd spent together.

Regali would not allow tradition to keep him from knowing his own

Oathson. He promised himself to place the child in a settlement close enough to his own lands that he could remain a part of his life.

The night lagged. Regali, eager to pack his gear and take to the road, found himself hard-pressed to bottle his impatience. He frittered time by concocting an herbal remedy for colic–just in case; next he practiced his levitation skills, his concentration squarely focused on the flickering tongue of a candle's flame. When the Newblood stirred and began to cry, Regali floated gracefully to the floor. He was surprised the dawn had not yet come.

The Newblood eased back to sleep while Regali collected most of his possessions and neatly placed them in sack that seemed far too small to contain all the items. Even at the completion of this task, he found darkness still besieged his tent.

Finding himself with nothing more to do, Regali clutched the satchel at his side and opened it. He spread a cloth flat on the floor, and took the contents into his grasp. With his hands cupped together, he shook a collection of bones and murmured a short incantation. Then he let the bones spill back onto the cloth. They tumbled and bounced before coming to rest.

Regali studied them a moment. His face soured. He reached down and swept the bones up in one angry motion, as if to wipe away the fate they proclaimed.

Regali retied the bonebag when a voice startled him. He listened intently, but all he could perceive were muted echoes falling like whispers.

Soon men's shouts penetrated his solace from the fields, their voices anxious, though he could not tell what words they spoke. As he tried to understand their calls, a most curious statement propelled him to the mouth of his tent.

"A black sun rises!"

## IV

Suspended in the East a most hateful and ugly celestial atrocity hovered over the horizon. A great black orb radiated a fiery shower of pitch, stirring those who beheld it to angst and panic. Like an evil brother to great Thulmuchi's brightly shining disc, it crawled and crept toward the heavens, spilling a pulsing demonic darkness more ebon than the murkiest midnight.

Frightened peasants ran screaming across the fields, crying out desperate prayers to their gods. Fires burned brightly in almost every quarter, as if those who raised the flames thought they might melt away the sooty darkness with their small sparks.

Regali spat out a curse. He did not know what power had changed the nature of the skies, nor what source of magick might change it back. Eyes would fall upon him and his brethren begging for answers; pleas would come to *right the benighted world.* Before he could give the matter further thought, he sought first to protect the Newblood; second, to find those Dassmen yet present so they might unite and face this unprecedented challenge.

Regali soon learned many Dassmen gathered in the great marquee of Denibaas. Under the canvass of this renown Dassman, and around a great table covered with trinkets and tomes, there sat more than a dozen potent practitioners of the Art. Some were able-bodied and athletic individuals, muscular, brawny, and brimming with youth. Others seemed frail and fragile, old, withered; but they too were powerful, able to out-spell any of their younger companions.

The one named Arcalius dipped his finger into a goblet of wine and stared down at the cup as though answers might wash up in the swirling spirits. His long, narrow face and head were crowned by tresses of white flowing hair. With a delirium of mingled bewilderment and horror in his countenance, his keen eyes sought omens and auguries amidst the ripples.

Unakepa of Odwolf'ld–ever the boisterous member of the crowd–argued with the red-bearded Yamasualtk, slapping his copy of Authok's Verses of Knowledge and spitting out various stanzas with unerring conviction.

Denibaas himself engaged Eralala the Warbreaker in a heated discussion, the only woman present, when Regali made his silent entrance. Eralala, one of five female Dassmen in all history, contended that only Tenvala'Aran was capable of performing an act of such evil, and that only with the aid of one of the Ancient K'Nwnmeir Masters could he have achieved this most heinous feat. Her opinion met with little acceptance as four nearby Dassmen chuckled shamelessly.

"Tenvala'Aran, that miserable worm spawned by the witches of the Ampehr Mires, would not dare set foot within the walls of Harchil; not in any season, not on any day, and certainly not during the Convergence of Oulahzu," Denibaas said. "I dare say that half the celebrants would risk torture and death, and break the Covenant of Oulahzu to bleed his worthless soul from his wretched body!" Denibaas grinned as he spoke, showing off his reddened teeth.

This tall, tan, and wiry man paced across the floor, wordlessly commanding the others to cease all discourse. It was clear with the passing of Sanggruth the Glum and Thoriitch of Nutt, Denibaas would assume the role as patriarch of all Dassmen.

"What other theories have you, *brothers?*"

"'Twas the doings of the Hidden Priests of Umon-Thummat," Unakepa, a young Dassman, spoke bluntly. "I set blame upon them for this action, and I needn't look any further than recent history for evidence to support my claim. After all, who was it that stole the Blackgem of Harchil nary a season ago? And what of the testimony given by Sir Nealuc of nightly offerings to the gibbous monstrosity that lurks in the Halls of the Moon?"

"Nay!" cried Cyhthus, a narrow-faced balding fellow. He wore a wreath of flowers about the rim of his sweaty head. "We look upon the act of some angered god. Not any one mortal, be they member of the Covenant or otherwise, has sufficient power to do this thing!"

"Hold your words," Regali called out, tired of the bickering. He drew aside the flap of the great tent, in spewed black rays. "Outside, the lands already wither beneath this menace. The people tremble and weep. The sky is blighted by a black sun. And here, inside this tent of Denibaas, we squabble, quarrel, disunite. Have we lost sight of our responsibility? Does it not rest with the men and women adept in magicks of many origins to set the lands, the people, and the sky right once more?"

"But Regali," Denibaas replied in a condescending tone. "We cannot end this nightmare until we are certain from whose mind it stems. Now, be seated and offer some of your own insights."

Regali sat amongst his peers, but found he had nothing to offer. He was at a loss for explanations, and simply could not conceive of the madness behind such an act. Peculiar, he thought, that only so solemn an occasion as this could draw together all the Dassmen outside of the Convergence of Oulahzu.

Within this fabulous shelter of Denibaas was gathered almost all of their kind—including the Newbloods. Many had lived considerably extended lifespans; at least two of those present would be as old as Sanggruth by the next Day of Repentance. Still, no matter their years, no matter their experience, Regali doubted any of them could match the four Great Essences which had recently passed over. Sadly, none even approached the wisdom of Sanggruth.

Regali took time to consider the aging tradition of Dassmen. It was his belief the lineage drew to a close. Their source of magicks was fading, their knowledge waning with each succeeding generation. The Dassmen were in decline, and another branch of the Alliance of Adepts would advance in energy as they faltered. The Dassmen could continue the line indefinitely, but with each batch of Newbloods their strength lessened and their wisdom waned. Regali foresaw their fold whittled down to one lone Dassman, carrying on their customs, endeavoring to complete the great circle that is their whole being.

"With one it began; with one, so shall it be done." Thus wrote the great philosopher-Dassman Tualksio more than ten thousand years past.

"I still hold confidence in my statements, for which I received from you all only scorn," shouted out Eralala, jostling Regali from his musings. "Why shrink you all from the likelihood that Tenvala'Aran was the architect of this Dark Spell? Do you all fear him so? Is it his bastard Dassman blood that causes you such agony?"

"Speak NOT with such insolence, Eralala!" bellowed Denibaas. "I'll hear that foul name spoken no more at this table."

"Denibaas," retorted the strong-willed female Dassman, "your apprehension is so readily revealed in your fury, it makes me laugh." A few men smirked. Others simply stared in astonishment. "Hear me now or I promise, you will not see the next Convergence of Oulahzu."

Though his power was probably greater than hers, never should a threat issued by any Dassman be taken lightly. Eralala, too, was silent, realizing afterward the seriousness of this confrontation. Before continuing, she sighed and scanned her fellow-Dassmen's eyes looking for allies, and hoping to discover no enemies.

"Now that I have your attention, I will continue," she said, her tone calm but penetrating. "We have spent half of this black morning brewing up ludicrous suppositions; some speak of gods, others of Hidden Priests, still others offer up the names of pitiful spellspeaks, charmers, and seers. Burning in the heavens is a *black* sun, and by the gods such a thing cannot be done by the waving of a wand, the rubbing of a ring, or the ordinary shedding of sacrificial blood. Something is strongly amiss in this country, and we all know but one man capable of compelling such acts."

Regali, like most of the others gathered there, had never encountered Tenvala'Aran. The tales whispered around campfires and the rumors spread by commoners provided good cause to avoid seeking an audience with him. Born from the womb of a High Witch impregnated by a renegade Dassman, Tenvala'Aran had earned his place as one of the most detested and abhorred malefactors in all the known realms.

"We must admit it—we fear him. I say it is Tenvala'Aran, whom we know to have access to all the wisdom of Dassman living or dead, and whom we know consorts regularly with imps, demons, necromancers, and murderous soulhoarders."

"I agree with Eralala," Regali said, adding weight to her argument.

"And to be successful at this venture, he undoubtedly came across some tool, some dusty old grimoire penned in blood, some old formulae for the conjuration of a sleeping archangel or granddemon. It is said such a man would be sensitive to the darkest icons of the forgotten ages when hideous things like Noisuls and Sisneunamah reigned over the barren wastes. And could he not have been drawn to the Avenue of Magicians during these past days to discover such an icon?"

"When I found Sanggruth the Glum yesterday, he seemed troubled by something he had discovered along the Avenue of Magicians," Regali said. "But what could it be that lent Tenvala'Aran the wisdom to do this?"

"I know not, but I ask you all one question: Did not each and every one of you, upon entering the White Gate, feel *something*? A power unrecognizable, terrifying, painful and noxious–yet irresistible? I felt a presence, though I knew not what caused it. And though it quickly faded, I find it haunts me now." She looked to Denibaas and saw he knew precisely what she spoke of.

"I, too, experienced it," Denibaas admitted. "I know now what caused it. Your impassioned speech has revealed it to us all, Eralala."

A great clap of thunder resonated so violently it shook the table and made the ground tremble. Screams, more horrid than those of before, rang out across the benighted fields. Screams not of terror, but of pain–deep and full of agony, rent from the very soul.

Regali, closest to the mouth of the marquee, reached for the flap. Before his hand could grasp the canvass, an intense wind whipped the tent from its poles. Upon this fierce gale rode the stench of burning flesh. Across the fields outside the walls of Harchil, the hellish squall swirled. As the black sun burned above, the grass and trees shriveled and bent in the breeze. From the East, a white light pulsed over the horizon. Beneath this eerie light, the Dassmen watched an army approach.

## V

"What in the name of all the gods …" Regali snatched up his Newblood and joined others in seeking to ensure the infants' safety. All of the Dassmen gazed in horror at the silhouettes of a hundred-thousand warriors mounted on horseback. This uncanny army descended from the sky, riding upon a great rock bridge. Its source was unseen, deep in the heart of the clouds. From this quarter came the ear-shattering, heart-wrenching wails of the damned; from the muddy skies came the putrid breath of some foul realm of the cursed.

Mortal men ran by the Dassmen shrieking, their skin blistered, hair falling out in clumps as though the wind accompanying this hellish army was itself poison. Some men who beheld the flash preceding the thunder were now blind, and helplessly they stumbled over the landscape in advance of the warriors. As the first wave of horsemen rode off the bridge and onto the land, the grass blackened and turned to ash as nearby trees burst into flame.

"Do you see who rides at the head of their forces?" asked Eralala.

"Aye," answered Regali. "It is he, Tenvala'Aran. He wears the garb of his mother's clan and carries the Skullstaff of Yoiuow. But who rides by his side?"

"That is the real power," replied Denibaas, shouting to be heard above the gale. "I recognize him now." Then Denibaas stroked his brow, rubbed his eyes and shook his head. He looked behind him once, not at his companions, but to the countryside not yet touched by the foul and killing wind. It was as if he silently bid it all farewell.

"He who rides with Tenvala'Aran is known as Sisneunamah. It is the same being of whom the earliest Dassmen, our eldest fathers, slew in battle ages ago. In that unholy war, our predecessors fought alongside mortals for they possessed little power in the face of Sisneunamah's army of corpses. More than a million mortals died on the fields. I have been told that in some places of Mistorel, the lands have not yet fully healed."

"We are more powerful now than they were then. Can we not stop him? Can we not put an end to this war before the first drop of blood is spilled?" Regali remembered the stories of Sisneunamah vividly; these were tales to chill blood and drive men mad. "There were but four Dassmen in those days; I now count fourteen standing firm on this heath; and though the Newbloods are not able to act, certainly the power of their very existence augments our own."

"It will have to be enough," said Cyhthus. He clutched the hilt of his ancient, charmed sword and drew it from its sheath, ready to lead the battle himself. "Make ready your weapons, brothers and sister. We haven't time to waste."

The reeking gale rushed over the lands like a plague, causing livestock to stampede, crops to rot, and men to weep. Bonfires lit by frightened peasants now whipped into uncontrollable fury and spread over the countryside unchecked. Grinning skulls gazed down from their mounts. These demon soldiers snickered and roared at the devastation. Every hoof-fall quaked the ground, as the very walls of Harchil trembled and cracked. Yet, fourteen Dassmen bravely stood their ground as the uncanny army marched on.

"Behold!" called out Eralala, directing everyone's attention to the White Gate. Through the tunnel vault charged another army, a mortal army, led by King Awtheav IV. "We shall not stand alone!"

"And a mighty army I suspect it shall be," charged Regali. That the mortals could so swiftly organize their forces impressed him, and it comforted them. "With all the visiting peoples of Mistorel, I would guess this army shall number in the tens of thousands."

"Aye, Regali … and look there, from the north; if mine eyes deceive me not, I see the forty clans of Umbragu." Denibaas howled with laughter in the face of the carnage that would surely erupt. "Who'd have thought Dassmen and neo-shamen would ever fight side by side on the pasture-lands of Harchil?"

All the Dassmen joined in Denibaas' brief laughter, though there was little humor in the situation. All fourteen made ready for battle, save one: Unakepa had been chosen to remove the Newbloods to a safe distance behind the walls of Harchil and out of harm's way.

Regali checked his pack. Within he found several hishimas, a set of tylak-beads, a vile containing yammot blood, and a small green sphere. The hishimas, small black cubes, their value never greater than on the battlefield. Tylak-beads were useless unless he retreated across a stream during the course of the day; then he could utilize them in the flowing water to ensure the enemy would not follow.

He smeared the yammot blood over his face and eyes for it served to heighten the power of his spells. Finally, he placed the small green sphere beneath his tongue, hoping that in the event of his premature death his essence would be transmitted to another Dassman.

Sisneunamah's army pushed ahead with no great sense of urgency. At their passing, the land moldered, vegetation ignited, and animals fell dead. Their ranks spilled across the bridge with no end in sight. The black sun, now on high, seemed to swell in celebration. Around it blossomed a great fiery-gray aura, a smoky ring of dingy soot. Clouds loosed a deluge of boiling rain, the consistency closer to tree sap than ordinary rainfall. It burned men's flesh and, more than one fool enough to taste it, dropped lifeless to the soil.

Enchanters worked feverishly weaving spells to protect the mortal combatants and their steeds. Lines formed before the walls of Harchil, proud defenders standing their ground. Standards and banners raised as the great warriors awaited the first clash of metal, the first charge, the first blow, the first blood spilled.

Archers readied their bows and shafts while men of the cavalry anxiously mouthed prayers. Knights clung to swords and maces, eyeing the approaching holocaust army. Dassmen, High Wizards of the many Secret Orders, Temple Sorcerers, neo-shamen, and even the Mesenna'Ala stood alongside one another, fanned out between the mortal forces before the legions of Sisneunamah.

The king brought his stallion to rest amidst the small band of Dassmen. Regardless of Regali's sentiment that the strength of the Dassmen was in decline, they were still widely regarded as the most advanced and skilled workers of the Art, and thus the king acknowledged them.

When at last the chiefs of the two massive armies were within earshot of each other, Sisneunamah raised up a pale bony limb, bringing the throngs behind him to a swift halt. He and Tenvala'Aran paraded out before their forces. Tenvala'Aran had never before looked so confident, so charged with energy. Those few Dassmen who faced him in previous skirmishes had always managed to exploit a weakness, and always defeated Tenvala'Aran, leaving his forces broken–though sometimes at considerable cost. On this day, however, he radiated with a kind of drunkenness, as though inebriated on the virility supplied by the conjured ancient at his side.

Sisneunamah's flesh, parched and withered, clung to the bones beneath. His scrawny, feeble limbs only emphasized a sunken chest, and his warhelm seemed to cause him great discomfort as it bore down on his shriveled body. There appeared to be no life in him, except for a smoldering in his eyes as they pulsated with a green glow. To stare into them for any great length invited insanity. Those brightly gleaming sockets attested to the powers hidden within, twisting the skeletal figure.

"You know my name," the impotent-looking, rickety carcass said. It dropped the cloak it wore, revealing its hideous, worm-chewed, diseased, and mold-covered hide. Ribs showed through tattered blue skin. At places, it seemed something with more than a worm's hunger had gnawed upon flesh and muscle. Yellowed teeth beneath blackened lips twisted his detestable face with a smile. "I am Sisneunamah, and I live again."

"You are a shadow of the man you claim to be–a pitiful ghost and by no means his equal." Denibaas spoke with care, trying to gauge his enemy's intentions. "But even the tattered bones and reanimated, rotting flesh of Sisneunamah is an evil too great to let walk the land. As our forefathers saw to your annihilation before us, so shall we see to the destruction of your army and the dissolution of your very being."

"Brave words, coming from a lowly Dassman," hailed the purple-hooded Tenvala'Aran. Raising a skull-topped staff, he continued with a howl, "Do you not recognize the Second Coming of Namolah? Can you not hear the shrill tittering of the army at hand? Or sense the swelling din even now erupting in the distant Holy Houses as demons cackle at and mock your hopeless attempt to stop him?"

"Sisneunamah was before beaten, his madness vanquished, and thought banished from these lands. His quest to awaken Namolah was not then, nor shall it be now, a successful one." Denibaas signaled to the other Dassmen; they drew together their thoughts, focusing their energies, and prepared to unleash their combined might.

"As you can see, Sisneunamah," Denibaas added, "in the days last our kind met with you, we were weaker and fewer in number. Look at as now–look at these twelve Dassmen here to face you down."

With that, a great blue fire swept up in a whirlwind and circled about the band of Dassmen. From the swirling blue fires shot steaming boulders, glowing red-hot, aimed directly at Sisneunamah. The attack clearly took their foe by surprise, and for a moment he seemed to waver in his conceit as the awful smile deserted his face. The spell startled Tenvala'Aran, too, whose steed bucked and reared.

But the boulders failed to reach their target, and with a sweep of Sisneunamah's gnarled forearm they fragmented and scattered.

The work of the Dassmen was far from over.

The ground beneath the enemies' feet trembled and pitched, as thunder rolled beneath the soil. With a force that made even the armies of Harchil and Mistorel shake, terrifying ivory daggers burst forth from the dirt, driving through man and beast—piercing armor as if parchment. From the opened bellies of horses spewed forth organs and blood, and amongst the legions of Sisneunamah great shrieks rang out. A forest of towering white spikes bloomed beneath the black sun, and upon each was impaled a soldier, horse, or both.

The battle had taken root.

## VI

With blood spilled, the armies surged ahead.

King Awtheav rallied his men with a battle-call. Sisneunamah sounded a trumpet calling his legions to action.

All voices fell silent, all prayers abruptly concluded with the thundering hooves of heavy horses pouring over the lands.

## Book of Being

Clouds of dust billowed up in the wake of the advancing hoard led by Sisneunamah and Tenvala'Aran. Regali could not begin to guess the number of foes bearing down on Harchil. As sure as light had been stolen from the day, so had all sense of hope been drained from his soul.

History and legend assailed the Dassman, and the tales of that earlier battle welled up to taunt him. It was true: There were more Dassmen now than there had been in that ancient battle; but it was clear that those early Dassmen possessed a much purer form of magick.

The dilemma could be likened to the aging of a common sword: A virgin blade in the hands of a master swordsman was a deadly thing; with time, it could even become more powerful as sword and swordsman developed greater comfort with each other; eventually, the sword would wear and its keen edge grow dull beyond the point of resurrection. When it proved no longer an effective weapon, the swordsman would have to replace it with a new blade–or fall victim to his reliance upon a weaker blade with which he had grown intimate.

Regali distanced himself from his apprehension. Magick was magick, power was power. Wielded properly, it would not fail those who put their faith in it.

The five generals of King Awtheav IV positioned their men deftly. They set up several lines of defense as they skillfully played out their strategies. Soldiers stood their ground and awaited further instructions. Not one among them fled the field. None flinched nor faltered when the enemy raced onward. They all stood doggedly, determined not to abandon their comrades nor their country.

Bowmen loosed their sharp, flaming arrows as the first volley rained a shower of death upon the oncoming army. As the screams rose up amongst the enemy, cheers rolled through the lines of the defenders. The mortals had pierced the heart of evil.

Then swords clashed as the warriors cut and thrust and hacked. Spiked balls of a thousand maces kissed foes' shields. Rage possessed the warriors, and steel struck at steel, flesh, and bone.

The pikemen rushed headlong into the ranks of Sisneunama, making war against mindless shells. These things, these long-dead corpses animated by some damnable magick, had been reborn through the blackest of sorceries and assigned but one task: to kill, and kill, and kill again. But these things did not fight at all like dead men. It was quickly learned among the brave defenders that the army of Sisneunamah fought with the fury of caged wolves and the skill of fallen war-gods.

At first it seemed these arcane knights could not be put down. Yet fall they did, when blades bit at them and arrows burrowed into their hide.

They died by the dozen when they were touched by the black-fire unleashed by Dassmen, and when they were struck by smoke-spears flung by the Temple Priests.

The Dassmen concentrated on the vanguard of the enemy's ranks. Their combined energies had generated fiery orbs of white light that acted of their own volition–they swept across the fields engulfing the foe, spitting out splinters of bone and armor.

Tenvala'Aran, too, utilized those strange forces at his to command. From a book clasped in his left hand sparked mysterious green bolts of lightning, felling a dozen men with each discharge. The fields were transformed into swampy mires, swallowing charging soldiers whole. And more frightening, many mortal combatants could not but gape as their flesh peeled from their bones though no wound had been sustained–the venomous rains disintegrating the living.

## VII

Through the long, dark day the fighting continued, until it seemed there would be no end.

The black sun lingered low on the horizon, an eternal night at hand. When, unnoticed, two men wearing heavy cloaks whipping in the wind, stepped onto the once green fields that enveloped the sprawling lands of Harchil. Around them glistened pools of lathered, crimson. They beheld heavily armored soldiers lying face down in the mud, their weapons clutched fast in their hands. The moans of wounded and dying warriors on the field drifted behind the walls of Harchil and mingled with the wails of widows. Fallen horses struggled to stand erect on twisted, broken legs.

A string of defenders, their faces grim, limped back toward the White Gate through which these two passed. These men, no longer able to fight, glanced briefly at the two Mystics' belated arrival to the battlefield. From the felled, streamed tears of pain, sorrow, and defeat. Their faces clearly avowed to the excesses of madness played out before them that day.

Most of the fallen lay caked in blood from the tips of their helms down to their spurs, with skin purple and torn. Some men in this somber procession fell along the road.

To walk among the dead and dying, choke on soot smothering the air, hear the scattering of flies hovering over corpses: These things they had to bear as they sought the place where the battle raged.

When they reached the plane, both armies fought amidst the carnage. The king's second son, now in command of Harchil's forces after the death of his father and brother, called for his men to move back and regroup. Only three Dassmen fought on, Regali among them, but their powers faded. Denibaas had succumb to a great black mist flowing from the strange book held by Tenvala'Aran. Eralala, blinded by a burst of witchfire cast upon her by Sisneunamah, fought on in spite of her sightlessness.

Regali saw the two figures approach and, believing them to be without weapons, hurried with his steed to their aid. When he drew nearer he saw that one carried a large, somewhat familiar book. And as Regali reined in his mare the two folded back their hoods.

Regali was speechless.

He stared, his eyes implored some explanation, his expression nonetheless one of eternal thanks.

Finally, he spoke.

"Sanggruth?"

"Aye, my son. And Thoriitch. We saw signs of this crippling evil, though it was not made fully clear to us until after our passing."

"How did you … you passed on, into …"

"That is correct, Regali. We have returned from the *Book of Being*." Sanggruth was not the same man Regali had accompanied a day earlier on the Last Walk. A smooth face red with life, his fingers no longer gnarled; he walked without the aid of his knotted staff, and his eyes shone with a power beyond that of any one Dassman. "There is but one way to defeat Sisneunamah, and we must do it ourselves. Take your fellow Dassmen and have these mortals clear the fields. Their work here is done."

"But surely you two alone cannot take on the whole of Sisneunamah's legions?"

"We are not but two, my son. Generations of Dassman stand with us, prepared to make the ultimate sacrifice," Sanggruth said. "Now quickly, clear the field."

Sisneunamah and Tenvala'Aran presumed victory was at hand as they watched their opponents march haphazardly off toward the walls of Harchil. Sisneunamah, no longer a crumpled old derelict, had been rejuvenated during the course of the battle. Now he appeared as a man in his youth with long, flowing, golden hair. He laughed and turned to his savior, Tenvala'Aran.

"It is with no small gratitude that I thank thee, Tenvala'Aran, for freeing me from my entombment and leading me on this noble crusade. Indeed, the day is won, the field littered with corpses, and I am fast-becoming my old self. I thank you for diving the location of my decaying form, finding the book that would allow you to rouse me from my slumber, and helping me call to arms my long dormant legions."

"In the name of Namolah, I would do anything."

"Then you shall offer up *The Namolah Blood Treatise* that I may animate the corpses of these soldiers which our forces have dispatched this day?"

"Certainly." As Tenvala'Aran passed the book to Sisneunamah, the blond-haired leader of corpses whipped his blade around and slit the rogue mix-breed's throat. Rasping, Tenvala'Aran coughed and wheezed, mouthing a single word: "Why?"

"Do you not understand? I've done you a great service to show my thanks. No more do I need your paltry magicks to aid in my conquest of these lands. Now you may serve me as a loyal soldier in my legions!" Tenvala'Aran slumped forward on his horse and spilled lifeless to the ground. Sisneunamah, a despicable smile blooming across his face, turned to his powerful legions and cheered: "And now, on to Harchil."

"Hold, Sisneunamah!" declared Sanggruth the Glum, cloak cracking in the vile wind. "You shall march no farther into this land. You shall not draw one more drop of blood. The First of the Four Dark Keeps which you seek shall *remain* in ruins, buried beneath the city of Harchil."

"Who are you, Dassman? Have you not seen the ire with which I have claimed your brothers and sister? You are no match for me."

"We are stronger than you realize, Sisneunamah," Thoriitch voiced. "We have traveled great distances in little time, and gathered many allies."

"Where are they, then? You stand alone before me ... weaponless and pitiful." Sisneunamah, irked by their insolence, lifted his brawny arms to lash out at them with a spell. But before a single word could be uttered, before the leader of legions of corpses gathered the energy to unleash his power, he found his arms stripped of flesh; the muscles beneath shredded and torn asunder. His bones crumbled, reduced to dust. Sanggruth and Thoriitch, the authors of this most potent spell, had not even moved.

"What magick is this?" cried out Sisneunamah, gazing angrily at the stumps of his arms.

"It is time you returned from whence you came and the book you hold is once again merged with its counterpart." Sanggruth opened the *Book of Being*. In a blinding flash, all of Sisneunamah's forces melted into the soil, venting only one throaty wail as they ceased to exist. "Though it was banished once, ages ago, from fear that it would destroy the *Book of Being*, it now must be returned; and along with it, you too shall be drawn in, Sisneunamah. After all, you are linked with the *Namolah Blood Treatise* as much as we Dassmen are a part of the *Book of Being*."

A tremendous flash shot across the landscape, trailed by a deafening shriek from which all mortals outside the walls of Harchil fell unconscious upon hearing. The afterglow faded until the only trace of it could be found in a pulsing aura enveloping Regali and the still-hidden Newbloods.

## VIII

Afterward, Regali turned his gaze to the battlefield. He saw nothing but scorched countryside where the three forces had battled.

After some time, Regali realized that Eralala and even Unakepa–who'd been watching the Newbloods–had vanished, perhaps caught in the vortex of the *Book of Being* due to injuries suffered during battle. He mourned the loss of his brethren, and prepared adequate ceremonies to mark the passing of each.

When he turned his attention to locating the *Book of Being*, Regali discovered it, too, had disappeared in the closing moments of the battle. He spent days scouring the lands surrounding Harchil, though at heart he realized the ancient tome had been sacrificed to ensure that dawn never again would come with the rising of a black sun.

But that also meant the book could never again spawn Newbloods, and would never again welcome the noble spirits of passing Dassmen. When Regali's time came, he would die like a mortal.

Though saddened by the passing of an era, Regali found he had little time to mourn. He retrieved each of the Newbloods, and with them he took to the merchant road to traverse the countryside. Tradition commanded that he find suitable parents to rear the four young infants, but Regali felt compelled to do otherwise.

Instead, he set out to raise the last of the Dassmen himself.

Lee Clark Zumpe is a reclusive author leading a life of obligatory asceticism in a two-bedroom, one-bath concrete-block cave-dwelling in the most densely-populated county of enigmatic and exotic Florida. He resides with his wife, his daughter and an embarrassingly extensive collection of Silver and Bronze Age comic books.

Afflicted at an early age with a compulsion to compose intricate, engaging falsehoods, Zumpe began scrawling out fiction and poetry to stave off inevitable madness. His work has been seen in magazines such as Weird Tales, Space and Time and Dark Wisdom, and in anthologies including Horrors Beyond, Corpse Blossoms, High Seas Cthulhu and Cthulhu Unbound Vol. 1. Zumpe is rumored to have a doppelgänger who has assumed his identity and who currently masquerades as an award-winning entertainment columnist with Tampa Bay Newspapers.

# The Birthing Blades

By Dale L. Sproule & Sally McBride

From a second story window, the curved neck of a streetlamp rose through the fog in the parking lot like the prow of a Viking ship. Neil heard church bells over the hiss of rain, and a rumble of faint thunder. The sounds triggered a chord in his brain–the first notes of a dirge, the birth of heavy metal–a soundtrack swirling up through the fog in his brain to remind him of his life *before.*

"Who is this, who stands behind me?" Neil sang, pressing his forehead to the cold glass. The words weren't quite right, and further lyrics refused to come. In that instant of distraction, he lost the melody, and when he dug for it again all he came up with was, "It's raining, it's pouring, the old man is snoring."

There was indeed someone standing behind him. The sound of her voice pulled his attention back into the room. His depth of focus shifted and he found himself staring at the silvery rain-patterns on the window pane–layers of dream peeling back to the bare framework of cold reality. He took a deep breath, feeling as if he'd just had a strong cup of coffee. Another deep breath, almost painful.

Reality.

He had known it well. It had never been kind.

"No," Neil declared. "The old man isn't snoring. He's waking the hell up. Isn't he?"

A nod from the young nurse, who cupped her hand under his elbow then guided him back to the bed.

"You need to focus. Look at the picture again."

In his hand was a photo in a sturdy plastic frame–himself with two beautiful women–his daughters! Hillary. And Daphne–who'd never been back to visit after bringing him to this facility. He hadn't recognized her, refused to come with her, unpacking his bags as she tried to fill them; finally, yelling at her to leave him and his stuff alone. She came back after dinner all red eyed and anxious, with some guy who introduced himself as the Director of Admissions at Upsilon Assisted Living. The memory was all quite surreal and not nearly as soft and warm as his underlying feelings toward Daphne.

Her last words lingered. "I need you to remember I didn't just dispose of you. We talked about you coming to live here, and you were aware that it was happening. I need you to remember I was here for you. That I … I said goodbye."

"I'm fine, honey. Of course I remember." A lie, but she seemed like a nice girl.

Hillary was different, visiting him every day she spent in Toronto, helping sell his house and sort out his affairs. Though it was awhile since he had seen her either.

"How long have I been here?"

"We've talked about this. The answer's inside you." She put her hands on either side of his face, her long cool fingers on his temples and cheeks.

He blinked hard, astonished he *did* remember.

Two months.

This nurse–Jaynie–somehow the blur of existence didn't engulf her like it did everything else. His mind grew clearer in her presence.

"Neil, I'm sorry, I didn't want to do this so soon. You're not ready yet. But we need you, *now*."

As he gazed into the face of the nurse who wasn't really a nurse–the air sang with the sound of a thousand feather-thin blades slicing through fabric. Threads snowed down as bladed wings rose up behind her. Her small, bare breasts held pierced nipples. A fierce smile changed her face.

"Do you remember Gallowrat?" she asked.

*A small, middle-aged man, nondescript, scared-looking.*

"The janitor?"

"Yes."

"Do you remember what you agreed to?" She froze Neil in her ice blue gaze.

"You're going to put Gallowrat's consciousness … into my body?"

Even knowing he was right, he shook his head at the absurdity of it. Clearly it was the dream that immersed him and reality that had been stripped away. He squirmed ineffectually, his mind trying to find an escape route from this stream of logic.

Half expecting to twitch his limbs and wake himself up, what actually woke him were Jaynie's fingers digging into his shoulders as she shook him.

"You have to be here for me Neil."

## The Birthing Blades

"But why me? I'm old, dying ..."

"You're one of the youngest patients in here. Early onset. Not even 60. And believe it or not, Neil, your body is actually in pretty good shape. Considering."

He saw himself in the dresser mirror behind her. With the slouch and the paunch and the man-boobs, he couldn't kid himself that he was anywhere near fit. He looked into his own face and barely recognized himself–the now crooked smile, eyes dull as stones. No mere Alzheimer's for him. Dementia with Lewy bodies they called it. He'd researched it when it was first diagnosed.

DLB could cause hallucinations, quite possibly as wacky as talking to a woman with wings. He blinked repeatedly, even pinched himself. This seemed so real–yet so impossible. It was too absurd to embrace, until embrace him it did.

Remembrance washed over him. This facility was no longer a refuge for the old and confused, but rather, a nest for the soul-eating creature in the basement–the barrow queen.

"I can't–can't do it. I'm not ready." But even as he said it, he knew there was no choice. No way but forward.

"Ready or not, here we go."

She kissed his nose and the corner of his mouth. He felt her hot, moist breath. A surge of desire ran through him, something he hadn't felt in years. She smiled and pulled away when he tried to kiss her back. "Now," she said.

The wings were gone–as if they were never there, the shredded garment back in one piece. Despite his permanent state of confusion, this was especially perplexing. He followed her across the hall, and she unlocked the stairwell. *If I trip, I might break something. Then I'll be no good to her. She'll leave me alone and broken–like everyone else in this place.*

The door at the bottom opened out into a nexus of dimly-lit concrete corridors. The warm, dank air smelled of bleach. Two sounds grew louder: a roaring and a screeching. *A broken clothes dryer? Someone being tortured in the furnace room?*

A shape emerged from a side door, blocking the passage before them. Neil recognized her as the bossy, sarcastic supervisor from the patient lounge–usually staid and strict, now grinning like a maniac as she advanced, hips swaying.

"What are you doing down here?" she demanded of Jaynie. "And why have you brought a ... wait a minute. Funny how the deadheads start getting their memories back when they're around you. Damn it, I should have seen you coming."

"Maybe the senility is rubbing off on you," snapped Jaynie. "How old are you, really? How many human souls have you fed to Elophasia just to stay alive?"

The chunky, red-haired nurse's eyes widened as she raised her arms above her head, chanting in a reedy voice.

"From the lightless domain–" Her next line segued into an unfamiliar tongue.

Jaynie shoved Neil behind her, slamming him to the wall where he slid to a terrified crouch. His mouth gaped open as Colleen finger-painted the air with darkness. Like coils of thick smoke, blackness spun from her fingers toward them, stinking of burnt trash. Neil choked, lungs searching for breath.

A shriek filled the air as Jaynie's metal wings unfurled once again, showering him with sparks where they clashed against walls and ceiling, flashing over his head and past his face with a cold, soft whistle.

They cut Colleen off mid-word. For a frozen instant, the woman was made of ribbons of flesh, poised in the air as if Colleen herself performed some ghastly trick. Her coils of choking black smoke vanished as she collapsed into a bloody pile.

The air misted with a coppery drizzle that stung Neil's eyes. A haze of blood condensed on the overhead bulbs, dimming the passageway. He saw little more than Jaynie's silhouette. The air stank.

She bent down to him, taking his trembling hands and looking him in the eye. "This wall is an illusion. It conceals the Barrow queen's chambers. On the other side, we need to find Gallowrat as fast as we can. He's still alive, but the bond between us is tenuous. Elophasia has been growing like a tumour under this hospital for years."

The bricks took on the texture of flesh when Jaynie pressed her hands against them. Then the wall opened like a mouth and the two of them tumbled into a huge chamber.

It was like trying to gain footing in a bouncy castle filled with slime. The pillowy floor rose and fell with the slow, hot rhythm of breathing. The flesh-pink walls dripped. Instead of being affixed to concrete, Neil realized the lights here were free-floating and multiplying.

He stared at what appeared to be a small, flickering flame and saw within it a human figure, writhing. It sailed toward his face like a rippling torch, scorching across his forehead to his hairline before he dodged out of the way.

Jaynie's razored wings swept toward them, metal feathers flaring wide. One of the fire creatures dove, like Icarus under the wings, clawing for Neil's ankles to pull him down; but Jaynie's blades descended and cut its body into flickering particles. Her flapping wings clashed like swords as the wind they whipped up put out the remaining flame-creatures like candles on a cake.

The chamber howled, all surfaces writhing as Jaynie's furiously beating wings sliced repeatedly into its flesh.

"Oh God. Oh my God …" Neil tried to find the door they'd come through, but all saw were walls of flesh. The malevolence seethed around him. This was the queen Jaynie had talked about. Not a person, but a sentient room made of meat–alive and deadly.

Together they crept across the throbbing floor of the chamber, Jaynie peering ahead through the fetid air. Suddenly she leaped ahead, dragging Neil behind her.

"He's over here!" But before Jaynie reached him, huge daliesque fingers rose from the floor wrapping around her. Enclosing Jaynie in her own wings, it turned them into a bladed chrysalis in which to crush her.

"Go to Gallowrat! Get him out of here."

In her zeal, Elophasia forgot the blades were double sided. A deafening shriek filled the chamber as Jaynie twirled and the giant hand burst open in a mess of fluid, muscle, and bone.

The man who lay charred and moaning on the bloody floor did not look like the same person Neil met earlier that week. In fact, he was barely recognisable as human: every inch of his skin flayed and charred, even his eyelids. How could he still be alive? Horror warred with pity. Pity won, at least briefly.

Jaynie scrambled over and knelt beside him, touching Gallowrat's lips with her fingertips as if to draw life to his surface and kindle it.

"I've brought someone, Rat. The new husk–the willing one. You have to hang on." Suddenly the floor buckled, tossing Jaynie back and throwing Neil down hard enough to wind him. As he lay gasping, she scrambled to his side again.

More than ever, he felt too old for this shit, but adrenaline surged through him and somehow he got the injured Gallowrat's arm over his shoulder. Amazingly, Gallowrat didn't fall apart as they lifted him. Neil was afraid to take a step, for surely a vast acid-filled stomach lay just beyond this giant throat.

Jaynie glared at him. "Come on, Neil! Pull yourself together or stay here and die."

Her flailing wings kept the peristaltic walls at bay until they drew in like bellows. Jaynie gasped as the walls collapsed around them.

"Be ready to run!" she cried. Her wings clashed and spread in the confined space, piercing the flesh in a hundred places then sweeping down, turning the flesh to confetti. Jaynie pulled them from the afterbirth-like morass onto the concrete floor of a corridor.

"Did you kill her?" Neil panted, too tired to even get up, let alone try to carry Gallowrat.

"No, damn it. Since her flesh isn't of this world, this wound isn't real. The metaphysics in magic can be kind of twisted. But I do think she's hurt. We may have time to get away."

They dodged into the first stairwell and laid their burden down at the bottom of the stairs. An insurmountable obstacle. Trapped. He looked down at the charred wreck of Gallowrat, struggling for every breath.

Jaynie's voice was soft, sad. "With your body and his magic, we have a chance. Take his hand, Neil." She turned and ran fingers along the edge of the door, singing in another language–the language Colleen had used just before Jaynie had diced her. He sure hoped her spell was more potent than Colleen's.

"Will I still be here after Gallowrat … moves in?"

She smiled and stroked his cheek. "Yes, but I don't know how much of you will be left. You'll be sharing your mind and body with someone else. We should be able to control your disease and get your synapses firing properly again, at least for a while. But magic can't repair all of the damage, nor can it prevent the dementia from eventually claiming you again."

"How long will I have?"

"Years. Decades maybe. When Gallowrat moves into your body, you'll be there to guide him. You're familiar with your own body and how it moves and speaks–the connections are already made. He won't have to expend magical energy to animate every muscle and organ like the queen's imps have to. You'll be much stronger than them. It's like repairing a dented car as opposed to one that's completely rusted out."

Neil shook his head. "Then why doesn't Elophasia do what you're doing? Leave a soul in the body as a host?"

"She'd starve without the souls to feed on. And even if that weren't true, she'd have a hard time finding willing hosts. Most people don't want to share their bodies. A host body taken by force simply dies and becomes a vessel. Its soul either flees or is consumed. I wish I could explain more but we have to do this, *now.*"

The dying man's hand was hot, scabbed with burns. A surge of tingling warmth tickled, then bit into Neil's palms and fingertips.

Jaynie bent over and gave Gallowrat what appeared to be a long kiss. Her back arched as she held herself over him, careful not to touch his raw skin. She lifted her head, a delicate trail of smoke streaming from Gallowrat's lips to hers. Then, taking Neil's other hand, Jaynie leaned in and kissed him. Her lips were soft and warm, tasting of smoke and tears and blood. He savoured it as long as he could.

Gallowrat's essence flooded into him, filling his body like water seeping into an edifice of sand. It was expected, but still a shock. Gallowrat's voice in Neil's head was sexless.

The entity called Gallowrat had been a woman as often as it had been a man. Neil saw a crowd of faces, milling, and heard voices of people he had never met, but he knew them–many of them intimately–countless people, of all ages, races and genders. As an imp, Gallowrat had dwelt in husk after husk, serving his barrow queen. But he'd managed to grow a soul, due entirely to a relationship with another barrow imp who'd been reborn beside him through dozens of iterations.

When Jaynie had arrived and offered them a chance to live out their days in a normal relationship, they'd jumped at it. But when Gallowrat's mate died, he gave his loyalty to Jaynie.

Now the imp's voice was in his head, permeating everything–simultaneously rumbling and cooing, vibrating in his skin.

*Welcome to me, welcome to we, welcome to us.* They were different voices, yet the same–a flood of half-memories washing through Neil/Gallowrat's mind.

Neil gasped as Jaynie's fingers dug into his shoulders. "Is it done yet? Is the merge complete? We have to go!"

He heard a slamming noise, only gradually recognizing them as gunshots. They were throwing conventional weaponry into the mix, along with magic. The vertical window on the door shattered.

"They're using lead!" Neil heard himself shouting to Jaynie. "They think it'll hurt you." The words came out of his mouth without him even being conscious of forming them.

Finding someone else controlling his actions in even so small a way was extremely disturbing. He found himself mentally pushing against the intrusion, trying to take back control. His heart pounded and his limbs went to jelly. He leaned against the wall, hyper-conscious of his own heartbeat, his breathing.

*We'll merge eventually*, said Gallowrat to Neil. *But in the meantime, I need you to let me drive. Are you okay with that?*

Already knowing Neil's answer, Gallowrat smiled at Jaynie. "We'll be fine." She smiled back at him as he bounded up the stairs.

Before he reached the landing, their attackers cracked the magical seal on the door below and came through in a burst of gunfire.

Stepping out of the stairwell at the B-wing nursing station, Neil found himself looking into the face of a nurse he knew–someone who'd taken good care of him.

Yvonne was the same age as his own daughters–just back from maternity leave. As Jaynie reached the top of the stairs, a bullet ricocheted off her armoured wings and hit Yvonne in the upper chest. She fell back in her chair, silenced by shock. Yvonne would almost certainly die–or become a snack for Elophasia if she survived the crossfire. So, Neil reasserted himself–retaking control of his own body to keep Gallowrat from running right past her.

*We have no time*, said Gallowrat.

*We have no choice*, Neil replied, appreciating that their dialogue was at the speed of thought.

*At least let me do this* … Gallowrat didn't have to form the whole question before Neil relinquished control back to his new co-inhabitant and they dove under Jaynie's wings to tackle the imp firing the weapon.

Gallowrat knew what he was doing: heels connected with shins and the shooter's chin slammed into the doorframe. Toppling, Gallowrat took his handgun and turned it on the husky, ginger-bearded imp coming up the stairs. As the bullets hit the new attacker in the chest, a ghostly version of him shook free and floated away.

*Which is what happens when a barrow imp truly dies,* Gallowrat shared, but Neil had already figured it out.

"They're coming from every direction." Jaynie cursed as he turned around. "We can't take them all on …"

The switchboard was almost certainly under Elophasia's control, but seeing Yvonne's cell phone on the desk, Neil asserted himself again, picking it up and dialling 911.

"There's a shooting at Upsilon Assisted Living," he said, then set the phone on the desk with the screen still glowing.

"The last thing Elophasia will want is for this place to fill with police and reporters," Gallowrat said to Jaynie. "They'll have minutes to clean this mess up. Might distract Elophasia from chasing us." Several bullets thunked into the desk beside his face and he winced, before realizing he could shoot back. "Or not."

As Jaynie had warned, imps converged from all directions.

Yvonne was unconscious and Neil more weak and exhausted than he'd ever felt before. But he also felt Gallowrat's magic churning inside him. He pointed at Yvonne. "We can't just leave her here."

With a nod, Jaynie lifted the larger Yvonne as if she were a child, then spun, her wings flaring out. Like an oblong streamer, she began to twirl, spinning across the floor toward the window.

"Don't shoot!" cried the voice of someone wise enough to recognize that their bullets would bounce right back at them–a brusque and burly orderly whom Neil had always pegged as a bully. His lack of empathy suddenly made sense.

"We have to use magic," said a voice from the hallway.

A crackle of lightening lit the passage, but the bolt deflected off Jaynie's wings as easily as bullets, reducing a desk to splinters. Imps dove for cover.

"The queen is coming," said a patient, who was clearly not what he seemed.

"The queen is coming," affirmed the orderly.

"The queen is here," said the queen, taking over the husk of the only imp between Gallowrat and the window Jaynie smashed through in a hail of glass.

With just a few words, Elophasia cast a spell that made the air as thick as epoxy.

Microseconds stretched into seconds. Gallowrat opened his mouth to unleash a spell but knew he'd be dead before the words came out. Elophasia had already beaten him once. Even at full power, his magic was no match for hers. At least until Neil remembered he was holding the gun and squeezed the trigger.

It was true the bullet moved in slow motion, but with the hail of glass streaming at her from one side and the bullet from the other, the Queen had no choice but to abandon the husk, thus breaking the spell and giving Gallowrat time to scoot out from behind the desk and run toward the broken window. But he slowed as he approached it.

*That's a three storey drop! I can't!*

*We have to*, said Gallowrat, even knowing they hadn't recovered enough to survive a fall like this.

They jumped anyway. Neil screamed in fear. But in the split second before hitting the ground, something swooped in from the side, hitting him like a train and knocking his breath out of him.

Jaynie!

He clung to her, hoping his heart wouldn't explode. Her giant wings began to beat.

She laughed, whether at him and his panic, or for the sheer joy of escape, he didn't know.

As they flew toward the gate, he remembered Yvonne and said her name.

"She's on the grass. First thing the emergency vehicles will see when they get here." As though summoned, a police car squealed around the curve from the street, followed by an ambulance.

As Jaynie landed in the park next to the hospital, she asked, "Why did you go back for her, Gallowrat?"

"It wasn't me." He found himself grinning. "Well, I helped I suppose."

Struggling to assert himself was a bit like pushing through a crowd of invisible people, but Neil said, "I couldn't let her die."

"Because you knew her, or because she's an innocent?" Jaynie asked.

He shrugged. "She has a baby. I've seen pictures."

Jaynie stared at him and finally smiled. "I hadn't imagined there'd be this much of you left, Neil. Or that you'd be this strong, wilful even. You almost sacrificed everything I came here for." She was referring to Gallowrat.

He shrugged. "That's what you get for leaving me alive in here."

Her laugh surprised him. But it was short and sharp, followed by a long sigh. "Too many of Elophasia's imps are still alive. Her barrow too strong for me to fight alone. You and Gallowrat need to meld. Properly. Completely. I sense that with you, it may take some time."

As the sun rose under a shroud of blood red clouds, he considered her words. The air was cool and fresh, so different from the stale air of the common room, or the stench of the basement they'd escaped. Neil drew it in.

"That was a neat trick with the telephone, by the way," Jaynie said.

"What? Dialing 911?"

She nodded, "We'd never have thought of it."

He grinned, realizing how magical and inscrutable twenty-first century technology was to these creatures.

As she chanted some words in a language that was not quite English, Gallowrat told him, *she's casting a glamour spell to conceal our true appearance.* Which made Neil suddenly realize that she was naked and they were both covered in blood. Or at least, they had been just seconds earlier.

"So, what now?" Neil asked no-one in particular.

"Now, we get out of here," Jaynie said, as she took his hand and walked with him across the field. "You should have held onto the cell phone. Could have called us a cab."

Dale L. Sproule's fiction has appeared in Northern Frights, Tesseracts, Pulphouse, Ellery Queen's, The Colored Lens, The Exile Book of New Canadian Noir and more than 30 others. His collection Psychedelia Gothique features 17 of his best.

He has written about horror fiction for Rue Morgue and about SF for Books in Canada, Parsec Magazine and AE Sci-Fi. Through the nineties, he co-edited and co-published TransVersions with Sally McBride. As an artist, his illustrations have appeared in over a dozen publications and his sculptures have been shown and won awards at conventions, including World Fantasy. He has nine Aurora Award nominations in four different categories. His work in every medium is obsessed with myth and archetype. You can track down most of his work through his website at http://dlsproule.blogspot.ca/

Sally McBride's novels Indigo Time and Water, Circle, Moon are available from Amazon and other venues. (An earlier novel, Remnants of Fear, is undergoing revision and is currently unavailable.) Her short stories and novellas have appeared in such magazines as Asimov's, Fantasy & Science Fiction, Realms of Fantasy, Northern Frights, Tesseracts, and many more magazines and anthologies. Her novella "The Fragrance of Orchids" (Asimov's) won Canada's Aurora Award and received Hugo and Nebula nominations. She has taught fiction writing and edited speculative fiction. Born and raised in Canada, Sally lives in Idaho with her husband and cat.

# The Knot

By Barry Charman

Five red rings surrounded the planet in a chokehold. The lingering trace of a terrible impact that had forever scarred the world and its people below. With each survey, further atmospheric wounds were revealed. The rings were the sign of an environment turning on itself, a disaster unravelling generation to generation.

Collectively they were known only as the Retch.

Staring pensively at the monitor as the ship began its descent, Cassidy wondered what the other captains before him made of the same view. What had they thought as this world rushed toward them? Did they have better plans, better ideas than him?

He looked across from his command section, to study Deena. He wondered what it was about *her* that was supposed to make this mission any different than the others?

There was a phrase in this system; *pawn takes pawn*. You come here on orders you don't understand, to communicate with a species who can't speak, and you never come back. You're nothing but a footnote on a dossier landing on someone's heavily polished desk.

*What's it all for? Is this a humanitarian mission, or are we all part of some cynical enterprise we'd never even understand? Is there something else down there that someone wants?*

*Like we'd ever know.*

Cassidy's stomach clenched at the swoon of the landing spiral. He made a fist and bit his lip, eyes bulging as a wild urge gnawed at him. *Give orders for targeting.* Fighting it down, he swallowed hard, as if the thoughts were a secret part of him he could consciously conceal. He had no illusions to this, however.

Dorian's voice came over the comms, "Planetfall in ten."

Concentrating on the mission rapidly unfolding, Cassidy mentally drowned out the countdown. He stared at Deena, her pink hair tied back like a cascade of frozen lava. How old was she? Twenty? Twenty-one?

What difference could *she* make? She couldn't possibly know what she was doing. Was she supposed to be an *advantage,* some difference-maker between life and death?

*Drown it.*

"Three … Two … One." A jolt, and a blizzard of atoms blasted away from the surface as *Mockingbird's Method* came to a rest.

*Well then. This is where we've come to die.*

Cassidy imagined himself laughing, then felt a surge of terror as he wondered if he'd made the sound aloud. Had it slipped out?

He looked around, no one stared back at him.

Exhaling heavily, he bit down hard.

Closing her eyes, shutting it all out, Deena visualised the henna tattoo on the back of her hand. Tattoos fascinated her, the temporary and the permanent. The idea that people held such conviction in things that they would carry images and words on their skin for all time told her people were stories wanting to be read. It told her everyone had a story to tell.

Even her.

They'd told her she was ready, but she didn't *feel* it. Maybe no one ever felt it; maybe they just got on with it, dove straight in.

Did she believe that?

Diagonally across from her, Cassidy sat spine-straight in his seat. She admired his posture, his control. She fidgeted. Even though she was held tight, her body felt uncoordinated, detached. Sometimes she stole a glance at him, to reassure herself someone was in control and it wasn't her. She opened her eyes, and there he sat, staring straight ahead.

*They're depending on me.* No one truly knew if they could communicate, not until they tried.

This was the tenth mission. The fact they had virtually no data from the previous nine, was a shadow behind her every thought.

She shut her eyes again, and went through some calming techniques her sister drilled into her. *They'll come in handy, when you're out there on your own*, she'd said.

She'd been right. She was always right. Deena smiled at the thought, she never usually felt that way, but then distance gave you a certain perspective.

# The Knot

The last time she'd seen Meera they'd been at the spaceport. Deena had only a few frantic moments with her before boarding. Meera appraised her, smoothed her tunic down, and tucked a pink lock of hair behind an ear, while tutting at the colour. Then she'd given Deena an intensely brief hug, and whispered how proud she was.

Deena replayed the moment as the ship lurched before the planet cradled them. The mission passed from concept to reality. It was here, it was now. Deena felt paralysed. When they came to ask her how she wanted to proceed, she'd have no idea what to tell them.

She felt sick.

Cassidy decided to just get the hell on with it.

Red lights blinked then turned white. He unstrapped himself, rose, and walked to Deena.

"You ready?" he asked, hoping he didn't sound as gruff as he felt.

She looked up at him.

He felt the blood drain from his face. She *knew*. What did she know? What the hell was wrong with him?

Twenty-one years old and she didn't give a damn. He wanted to scream in her face, wanted to be–

*Drown it.*

"Well?" he croaked out.

"Yes."

"Yes what?"

"I'm ready."

She deactivated the straps, but she just sat there studying him. Cassidy turned his back and got the hell away from her as quick as he could. Anger churned him up inside. Why? What good would that do him now?

Chen stood over at one of the monitors, doing a preliminary scan of the surface.

"How's it look?" Cassidy asked, desperate to keep his thoughts together, and off other notions.

Chen glanced up at him. "They've sent a meeting party."

"How many?"

"Dozen, maybe more. I don't think they're armed–"

"Ofcourse they're not armed, they've got to *dance* first." Cassidy glared at him, then abruptly turned away, needing to get some space.

*Space? I need to get off the planet.*

Deena breathed slowly. She still lingered in her seat, staring at the space Cassidy had commanded and abruptly vacated.

*I just stared at him.* She couldn't think of anything to say, and winced at her foolish, two-word answer.

Matthias suddenly appeared, "They're outside. We need you."

She nodded. No more time.

Pushing herself out of the seat, she wobbled unsteadily as she adjusted after the descent. Matthias nodded over at a terminal and Deena activated the feed. They'd sent a party to meet them. To *address* them.

If she didn't understand, if she couldn't make their intentions clear, things could get bleak fast.

"You ready?" Matthias asked.

She had her back to him and risked closing her eyes. They all wanted encouragement. She busied herself at the screen and mumbled some vague affirmation, not turning to see if he was still there. On the screen, the meeting party assembled in a semi-circle at the end of the docking bridge. While the bridge itself was covered, the land beyond was not, and the party simply stood there, waiting. A light breeze billowed the simple white robes of their Emissary.

None of them could speak. They used movement as language. Signs, dance, expression. These were their methods. All because of the Retch.

She stared at the Emissary. He was too far away for his face to be clear, but his posture spoke nonetheless. It was calm, refined. The subtleties of the dance were so intricate though; Deena remembered a teacher of hers who'd described it like a key going into a lock. The permutations of movement release everything that has to be said.

Deena wanted to study them at leisure. To marvel, to appreciate. But there was no time.

What happened now was simple: communication or excommunication.

Cassidy listened to all the activity. Everyone moved, preparing for the hatch opening, the moment the two groups met.

*No.* The word impaled his mind. Cassidy tightened up, like a tree about to be uprooted. *We're all going through the motions towards our deaths*, or so it felt. Wouldn't it be braver to admit that? To react to that logic?

Instead, he and the crew put on false smiles to greet their killers.

Madness.

He looked around and wondered where the girl was. *She must be good or they wouldn't have sent her.* But even then, did he really believe ideas could be exchanged through the right *movements*?

What if she made a mistake? No, what about *when* she made a mistake? It was inevitable, surely?

Laila walked over to him, tapping a finger against her sidearm. She appeared as agitated as he felt. He wondered if he covered it up better than her.

"What do you think?" he asked, keeping his voice low, but allowing a blunt edge to his words.

If the directness surprised her, she hid it. "If she can't talk to them, how long do we have?"

Cassidy gave her a military smile. It conveyed that this conversation was not allowed, and the absurdity of that was not lost on him.

"Just standby. If it falls apart, I'd like to think we'll be taking a few of them with us."

She gave him a resigned nod. "Couldn't we just fight back to the ship? Evacuate?"

"Sure, we can try." He didn't trust himself to say any more, so he slipped away while she looked uneasy.

As he searched for Matthias to relay final orders, he noticed Deena over in a corner. Her eyes were closed, as she practiced gestures in the air. A flow of delicate motions, punctuated with her small hands, long fingers, lithe arms. Her movements weren't so much graceful, as practical, a flurry of nuances that connected into some unfathomable passage of words.

She'd studied the tapes, learnt the culture from satellite images, but all she had now was instinct. He watched as she pulled her elbows in to her waist and brought steady palms up before a still face. She made fists, then quick fingers darted out, dancing one by one, before hiding, darting out of sight. It was a strange display; he wondered what she was saying.

Her poise, her control, impressed him. But he wondered if she had any understanding of the danger they were in. Was this all some metaphysical exercise for her? Some sojourn that enabled her to practice in the field?

Was she in control of it, or was it in control of her?

Deena breathed and tried not to panic. She felt the erratic movements of her fingers flutter before her face. It was an exercise she'd been training with, the movement was meaningless, but it connected her, it centred her.

*The roots provided for the leaves. The leaves, no matter how beautiful, were nothing but for the roots. The roots you never see, but it is they that must be praised for the tree.*

She recited the words. They gave her no confidence. But that would come, she hoped.

Feeling a tap on her shoulder, she opened her eyes. Laila stood over her. "It's time."

Deena nodded.

They exchanged nothing further. Deena stood and the other woman helped her into a lightweight atmosphere suit. It didn't restrict her at all, she knew some of the earlier teams had been handicapped by more cumbersome suits. She'd made sure she had something better.

As the team assembled by the hatch, Deena ran through her instructions. She tried to open herself to intuition and instinct. *Let them speak to me. Listen first, then answer.*

As the door behind them closed, and the air whispered before settling, Deena realised her hand shook.

The door in front of them hissed open, slowly bathing them with the pale light of another world. Deena had visited a few of the outer colonies, but she'd never experienced a moment quite like this. She looked around for some sort of reassurance, and discovered Cassidy staring at her.

Mentally, she tried to control the shake. She gave Cassidy a brief smile, which she hoped didn't look foolish, then turned and looked at the exterior door as it fully opened with a low whoosh.

Deena's mind was all over the place. She couldn't pin any of her thoughts down. Her mother's garden came to her. She imagined herself as a girl running through the tall flowers, their heady scent almost sticking to the air. Then she saw her mother dancing, before she'd stopped to teach. Deena remembered watching her through a window as she twirled and struck poses, like some doll brought wonderfully to life. She felt Meera's hands in her hair, making her first plait, remembered her sister's hands dancing on hers, with the first henna she'd taught her.

Then she saw her own small room at the academy, remembered a breeze ruffling fine curtains … That breeze was from another world too.

*Focus.*

Cassidy activated a communicator on his collar and whispered, "We're going out."

Deena's hand continued to tremble, so she made a fist, and felt her fingernails stab into her palm. She instantly unflexed. There must be no blood on her hands. The hands were a part of the language to come.

The body must speak for her. She saw this thought, clear, and *true,* and she held onto it.

Cassidy stepped out last. He tapped his collar, "We're out. Close her up." He heard the door shut behind him, but didn't trust himself to look. The image might provoke something.

Across the stone bridge, the welcoming party stood and waited. Cassidy stepped forward, while the rest of their small party crowded warily together. He nodded at Matthias, and then Deena. "We'll go forward."

She nodded.

"This is where you take over."

She nodded again, which galled him slightly. But then he realised her thoughts were no longer on him, she'd geared herself up for the communication and left them behind; now she was thinking only about the people across the bridge.

How could you trust someone so unafraid?

"Alright." Cassidy gestured with his hand for Deena to go first. She seemed to hesitate. He tried not to feel paranoid as she fumbled over protocol. "Move," he said, quietly.

She started walking. Cassidy stepped in behind her, flanking her on the left, while Matthias took up the right.

Ahead, the white-robed figures watched their progress.

The species had no language, so were known by no clear name. They were called the Dancers by some, but most called them the Retch, connecting them to the rings that had ruined their world, while also judging them for how they'd reacted to everyone who'd come before. Some said it was fair; others said it was cruel. Cassidy had no opinion either way.

He wondered how many more of the Retch were watching them, concealed, how many guns were watching them?

*How had they killed who they'd killed?*

They came to a stop before the Retch. Their Emissary, the dancer who was also their *speaker*, stepped forward. And then he "spoke".

His white robe fell away from him, billowing like a sail before fluttering to the ground. A slender body was revealed, dotted with small un-intrusive tattoos, marks of rank and station, affiliation and family. His legs and arms were bare, but for a white cloth that wound around his limbs. With hair cropped short, his features were almost wild. As he moved, expressions darted across his face as if naked and unashamed.

The dance began. The man pirouetted with raw emotion and stunning athleticism, spinning on the spot, ending in a still but strangely contorted position. His hands pointed in the air, and this was where ambiguity cost lives. It could have been a gesture of supplication or prayer. He could have been giving thanks to the sky that had brought them, or pointing as if wishing they would dive back into the sky that had let them through.

All the while, his face twisted. Eyes seemed to roll. There was nothing to latch onto, no one emotion, nothing *human.*

Even so, Cassidy knew what it meant. They were going to die.

The speaker danced. Or the dancer spoke.

Deena watched every movement, and tried to mentally mimic it, to understand it from the inside out.

When the first part of the dance finished, the Emissary froze in place, pointing to the sky like a statue. He wasn't looking at her, so she wasn't sure if he expected her to respond.

Then, in a movement so sudden she took a step backward, the Emissary spun back, as if reversing his movements, until he ended in a crouched position, perched on one knee across from her. He raised his head and studied her.

*The sky– no, we are from the sky– no, go back to the sky, no, welcome from the sky– no–*

She tried to understand what was expected, but where was the context…

Then she saw it.

*Forget everything else. The only context is us.* His dance was for her alone.

She stepped forward quickly, and pointed with one hand to the sky. She then brought her hand down, and threw both of her arms wide, before slowly bringing them together before her. The two hands touched, palms flat against each other. Then she pointed to the ground.

*We have come far.*

She ended the movement by pressing her palms flat against her side and stepping back. Behind her Cassidy hissed.

Deena ignored him. If the Emissary didn't understand, none of them would live long enough to argue over it.

The Emissary rose, then brought his hands together, the fingers interlocked, writhed–

The rings. The Retch.

He spun and threw himself down.

Their dance was contained to a black square of stone, upon it lay a cloth, a drape covered in lines and symbols. There was little for protection if the dance brought you down hard.

His fists thumped his chest, this question/statement was personal. He spun down and tapped the ground, before reaching up, sweeping his writhing fingers through the air, and then bringing his palm down flat against the ground.

*You have come through the Retch. The thing that hurts us. Why are you here now?*

He studied her, waited.

She took a risk

Moving her fingers as he had, she lifted her hand so it was vertical, blew through the fingers, closed them. Then she brought her hand down.

*We can help you with the Retch.*

The Emissary was suddenly, utterly, still.

Cassidy froze. Something was wrong. What the hell were they talking about? What did she think she was saying? What had she understood, or *thought* she understood?

His mouth went dry, while his heart slammed viciously around in his chest. The Emissary remained still. The conversation paused.

Why?

The Emissary brought his arms up and wrapped them around his face in an uncomfortable looking contortion.

The Knot.

Cassidy had heard about this. Sometimes the Knot appeared. No one knew what it meant, or how to answer it.

Essentially, they were dead.

*The Knot.*

Deena smothered her initial panic. She tried simply to understand. Was he rejecting the offer of help, or had he not understood it? Or was this something entirely different?

Seconds yawned past. Deena froze. She closed her eyes and took a deep breath.

*There is only the moment.*

*We are strangers. We are discussing the Retch. We have travelled through it, they have suffered it—*

Were they sharing this?

She brought her hands up, knowing she had to say *something.* You do the training at the academy, you do the research on the flight. Now only instinct remained.

She made the Knot, and then she opened it.

*The Retch is a terrible thing. You have suffered it long.*

Other movements followed, they became increasingly fluid to her, increasingly obvious as one limb caressed another and the details unravelled.

*We are your friends. Trust us. We came to help you.*

When she stopped, the Emissary stared at her, perfectly still. She tensed. Had she done something wrong?

Suddenly, in one fluid movement, he fell forward to the floor, then rolled and came to a stop immediately in front of her.

Deena heard movement behind her. Matthias had moved his gun from one hand to the other.

The Emissary knelt for a moment, holding the gesture before breaking it by rising to his feet—his face inches from hers. Now that he stood closer, she guessed he was a little over six foot, just as she a little under.

His two arms suddenly lunged for her head.

*Oh God.*

Behind her Cassidy swore. But the Emissary's hands were suspended parallel to her face. Not touching her, but ready to, *willing* to.

She understood, and brought her hands up to his head and mirrored the gesture. They stood there, a cradle of limbs, and held the moment.

Trying to remain as still as the Emissary, Deena felt her chest rising as tense breaths slipped out. It was all about control.

The fingers around her head flexed, as if caught in their own dance. She could just see them from the edge of her vision. Their fluttering movement made her think of butterflies, and she wondered if they shared the species, or something alike, a piece of research that had gone unexamined.

The Emissary brought his hands back, and kept them horizontally at his chest. She brought hers down until they were parallel to his, and then he moved his hands around hers. He pushed her hands together, his left palm above, his right palm below.

The hands closed.

*We accept you. Welcome.*

Deena breathed out.

After a moment, the Emissary stepped back, turned to the others of his party, and made gestures to explain.

Cassidy's face twisted with every movement he witnessed. How the hell could they ever trust these people? This mission was madness. They were just wasting time until one of them slipped up and confused the other. It was *inevitable.*

He realised that word had stalked his thoughts ever since they landed. If it *was* inevitable, then surely the smart thing would be to act first? Not just stand there, languidly waiting for the blow to come.

Did the conversation even matter if they already knew the outcome?

Deena came over to him, she beamed stupidly. "I think it's okay." How the hell could she think that?

"Okay?"

She nodded.

"What did you say?" *Did she even know?*

"I told them we were here to help them. I think he understands. The Knot is about the Retch, the journey. It's a gesture of unity. Acceptance."

*Acceptance?* Cassidy felt the recoil of emotion on his face.

Deena faltered. "Sir?"

"Good work," he said, able to quickly redirect his thoughts. "And what did they say?"

She smiled. "Welcome."

*It's a trap.*

Cassidy nodded. "Good. What happens next?"

Deena glanced back at the Emissary. "I think we're meant to go with them. This whole ceremony is about understanding visitors, learning if they can trust them. Now that we've been welcomed, we can talk further."

Cassidy just nodded. Every previous team had failed at this point. There had been confusion. Violence. Death.

For a moment, Cassidy felt the scream vibrate his larynix; he looked around, surprised no one had heard it. *What's wrong with them? Why aren't they screaming?* Perhaps they were, perhaps they were.

And they were waiting for him to lead them.

"Tell them we'll come."

The welcome party led them in a procession across a series of narrow walkways to a structure, built into the side of the mountain the landing pad had been constructed on. The ingenuity of the people took her breath away. When the Retch stopped them speaking, they made their bodies talk. When the people came from the sky, they built a way to meet them.

Deena wondered exactly what they thought of the Retch, it was a constant reminder of the disaster that had torn out their voices, wrecked their world. The rings were a malignant source of contamination. W*hat did the people view them as? They could have become gods, hated, worshipped, or both; cruel spectres that they cowered from. Instead they seemed to defy them, spite them with everything they were.*

Of course, she realised, the people that came *through* the Retch had a lot to prove.

The landing party was led to a long narrow chamber. Its white walls were embedded with small glowing stones giving off all the light. They were decorated with ornate patterns and diagrams. It was a tapestry, Deena realised. It moved with such movement, such fluidity. The *dance* had evolved into a written form as well.

She found the Retch in the tapestry. A ring of fire that lacerated the sky, choking the dancing figures beneath. She thought of the filters they'd brought, implants that could aid them, or at least help their children if there was too much damage in the rest.

The centrepiece of the room was a brightly detailed table. Deena got comfortable. Matthias and Cassidy sat by her to either side.

"Is there going to be some kind of meeting?" Cassidy looked uncomfortable. His strength inspired her, but sometimes she glimpsed these strained cracks in his armour. This was much for one man to bear.

"They don't talk at the table. They don't *talk*. This room is for eating alone. No unnecessary movements, nothing trivial like conversation."

"Trivial?" Cassidy darted her a sharp look. Like he thought she was mocking the mission.

"Sorry, I mean they put so much effort, so much physicality into their speech, that words are never wasted, never used informally."

He considered her a moment, then gave a curt nod.

After that, food was brought for them. Matthias scanned it discreetly and then nodded. The Emissary watched them eat. Deena felt his eagerness to communicate. At first, she'd been intimidated by him, but now she saw he was probably not much older than her. This whole experience must have been just as fascinating to him. How long had *he* prepared? How nervous of mistakes had *he* been?

She smiled falteringly at him. Did they smile?

His lips made a movement that might have been a smile. She wasn't certain, but glanced away, unwilling to stare at him for long.

After the food, the Emissary led them to an adjacent chamber and danced something different than before. These movements were personal, more relaxed.

"What is this?" Cassidy hissed.

"Relief, assurances, hope ..." Deena put words to the motions, as best she could.

Cassidy stared. "Are there questions, or is this just some statement?"

"It's a gesture." It might have been a commitment, but she couldn't say that for certain.

"Could you talk to him? Personal, like this? Could the three of us be alone?"

*Alone?* Frowning, she didn't understand, but didn't question. She needed them to know they were right to put their faith, their trust, in her, in Cassidy.

He knew this already. She felt foolish. "Of course, I'll see what I can do."

She realised Cassidy was thinking far ahead.

Cassidy followed them from a short distance.

Deena and the Emissary couldn't talk, but gave each other little questioning looks.

*He's looking for ways to kill her. Points to maim her. Vulnerable spots. She can't even see it. She probably thinks he's flirting with her.*

Cassidy had a headache. Rubbing his temples, he felt slightly sick, but it was alright. He was no longer a passive passenger, but in *control* now. Inhaling, he relaxed. The air of the planet felt vaguely acrid, as if old, dusty. Since their arrival its taste became increasingly obvious. With prolonged exposure, they'd probably end up the way of the Retch. He bet they'd love that.

The Emissary led them to an open courtyard surrounded by flowers. They were tall and pale, and he leaned toward them as if curious. Deena considered them and smiled, which made the Emissary smile.

*Oh, he's so eager to please her now that he knows how unguarded she is. She's like cattle being given a tour of an abattoir.*

Cassidy unsheathed the knife. After the initial confusion, everyone would thank him. They might give him a commendation. The idea made him sick. He wasn't doing this because he wanted a reward. He was doing this because it was the only clear, sane option.

Then Deena turned.

She saw her mistake.

"No!"

Cassidy's face was wild, scared, feverish, but his body utterly still. The knife glinted in his hand. The blade pointed down, but his grip clasped so tight his hand looked white like marble.

Instinctively Deena moved between them. The Emissary turned, and Cassidy glared over her shoulder at him.

*He's terrified. Has been all along.*

"Please …" Deena understood words as well as movements. The one word, gentle, pleading, almost child-like, bought her time.

Behind her she heard the Emissary step back, she was thankful that he couldn't cry out or raise the alarm, and hated herself for it.

Cassidy inched forward. "Get out of the way." It was a shout the volume of a whisper.

"It's alright. We're alright. It's done, we're safe." She held her hands up, unthreatening, in the back of her mind she wondered if the Emissary read these gestures as something entirely different.

Cassidy's focus suddenly darted down, looking at Deena for the first time since the knife had emerged. "I have to."

"Why? What do you think's happening here?"

His eyes roved from her to the Emissary. They looked unsettled, unable to rest. "They're going to kill us like they did the others!"

"They're *scared*," she stressed the word. "We came *through* the Retch. Think about that. Those rings are strangling this planet. These people are in pain. And we just drift down like it doesn't matter. How do you think that *looks*?"

Gently, she brought her open hand up until it hovered over the knife. She didn't dare touch him. He wasn't looking at her, or the Emissary, his eyes were unfocused, staring into space. Could he even hear her anymore?

"We're all so scared of each other, but all we need to do is communicate, and we've *done* that. It's over."

She glanced down at his hand, it shook.

"We're the ones who made it," she spoke softly. "We're the ones who tried to speak, and they're the ones who tried to listen." She hoped that hit home. For too many generations this planet had caused bloodshed. And for what? Those damn rings, and the confusion, the distrust they'd scattered.

"It's too late." Cassidy's voice strained, as if the Retch had got a hold of him and choked the words as they came.

"No. *Never* too late," she whispered, almost soothingly. "*Never* too late."

Her hand was on his, and suddenly the knife moved. Cassidy stared down. Shocked by the knife, or that his hand had surrendered it?

She stroked his arm, hoping he wouldn't flinch, or try to take the weapon back. "It's alright. Look what it's done to us."

The Emissary had edged around them, suddenly he lunged forward and tore the knife from Deena's hand.

Cassidy watched everything happen in slow motion. All of his thoughts had fallen apart and he couldn't quite put them back together.

But she made sense. And it *was* over, wasn't it?

Then the knife glinted in the Emissary's hand. He glowered at the two of them. Deena looked shocked, she brought her hands up and tried to make a gesture, but the Emissary slashed at her. She flinched back, the knife only grazing her.

Cassidy saw a thin line of blood appear on her arm and snapped back into reality.

They had come *through* the Retch, she'd said. It was *it* that had poisoned them all. *It* that had killed so many people.

The Emissary edged away from them, if he ran, if he *told*—

She had danced them around the bloodshed, and he had thrust their hands back into the wound. Cassidy didn't think, he just dropped to his knees. He brought his arms up and made the Knot.

The Emissary froze mid-step.

"Deena," Cassidy called to her, "can you explain?"

"I–I don't–"

He thought of the cut. How the pain must be suddenly registering. In one more second all of this could fall apart.

"Tell him I'm *sorry*. Tell him I'm afraid. Tell him the Retch is evil, it makes us *do* evil."

She stepped in front of him, and then made signs Cassidy prayed the Emissary understood. Her hands shook, but made wide expressive arcs, her fingers trembled, but danced. She made the marks of tears on a face, and shadows on the mind.

Cassidy wondered how many years they'd all waited for a chance like today, a chance like the dance the two of them had danced. If he'd thrown that away, he might have doomed the planet to a thousand years under the Retch. He hoped they'd punish him, if it came to that.

Deena stopped moving. Graceful as she was, tall, lithe—her body had seemingly run out of words.

"So sorry," Cassidy pleaded softly, he rocked back and forth on his knees. He'd held the Knot for as long as he could, but now his arms fell to his sides. "Just scared."

Deena held her hand out for the knife.

The Emissary looked at her hand. His body tensed, as if readying for a burst of violence or motion, perhaps both. But he held the tension, unreleased. This was another Knot, internal, emotional.

He made a sudden decision, and stepped towards Deena. He brought the knife forward–

It vanished. Cassidy waited for the scream. Deena and the knife had *merged*. But then she turned, knife in hand. She came over to Cassidy and helped him to his feet.

"We can never speak of this," she said.

He wanted to laugh, but just held onto her.

The Emissary watched them, then made the Knot once more, and stared up to where the five rings of the Retch pitilessly maimed the evening sky.

Cassidy watched him. Deena had said the Knot was a gesture of unity, empathy; a symbol that both evoked and rejected the Retch. Cassidy saw something more, to him it looked nakedly like hatred, but hatred that was ultimately a *release*. Their Knot was made to be undone.

The Emissary broke the Knot, his body relaxed, as if his soul had made a fist. He looked at peace.

"Will it be alright?" Deena whispered from his side.

Cassidy nodded. "I see it. I *understand* it."

She sighed, and he heard the relief.

Finally, he'd *heard*.

On the small screen, Meera danced. The feed was from earth, buffeted by a ten-day delay. Deena grinned as Meera stumbled and fell down giggling.

She'd sent her first report back, and now everyone was celebrating. The recording from Meera was just the latest. Deena leaned forward and gently tapped the screen. On the back of her hand, the henna tattoo had long begun to fade. She saw in the pattern there the faint impression of love and family.

At first, she hadn't been sure what to include in her report. There had been mistakes, misunderstandings on both sides, but the Knot had been made, understood, and undone.

The screen stalled, Meera froze mid-dance, it was like a word held, suspended; a promise, a hope. Deena smiled. This world had been frozen for more years than she could imagine. But the word had been heard.

The feed resumed, Meera's smiling face took up the screen, their mother's voice registered in the background, laughing, but all too quickly stalling again–the word once more frozen.

Deena stared at the image, and tried not to think about the dance stopping, starting, breaking down. Not a dance at all, but a stuttering cycle–

She chose not to pursue those thoughts, and waited, with a smile suspended on her face, for the message to resume.

Barry Charman is a writer living in North London, England. He has been published in various magazines, including Ambit, Firewords Quarterly, The Literary Hatchet and Popshot. He has had poems published online and in print, most recently in Bewildering Stories and The Linnet's Wings.

As a writer he is interested in various mediums, and has also published plays as well as flash fiction. An avid writer of flash fiction, he loves the craft and precision that comes with its discipline and limitations. He is currently working on a collection of poetry, as well as a novel for children, among other things.

He has a blog at http://barrycharman.blogspot.co.uk/

# The Hard Stuff

Philip Bran Hall

My name is Brendan O'Flaherty. I'm an alcoholic. I've been sober for three years, but you know that because you're all still alive to listen to my testimony.

You know, looking back I can hardly remember a day when our mission went right. Didn't we all go through the quarantine and the medical examinations, like always, before an interstellar voyage?

We did. There were a dozen different scanners; we were pushed and poked and prodded by instruments sharp and blunt, had fluids of all kinds extracted and injected, drips and electrodes attached and inserted in so many places it makes me wince just thinking about them. Don't ask me how Connie Leandros managed to conceal her malaria through it all.

I guess space crews are like football players–we play through pain rather than lose our place. Competition for mission berths is fierce. Go sick just once and you put doubt in the minds of those brainless file pushers back in personnel who're comparing you with supposedly healthy colleagues.

Pilots are the worst, so they are. Everyone wants to be a pilot. Every new recruit applies for pilot training just as soon as they engrave his first dog tag. The odds against being selected for flight school are maybe a couple of thousand to one; against making it through training, maybe five to one; after that you have to get an assignment. You don't *really* have to kill for a job, though it would help. What you must do is cover up your personal problems. Like all the others, that's what *I* did.

*Cassiopeia* originally carried five pilots. On a round-trip there's a lot of opportunity for personnel attrition, but five is usually enough.

Not this time.

Before we even intersected the orbit of Mars, Connie was confined to sickbay. Turns out the medical supplies contained no malaria remedies. You aren't supposed to get bitten by mosquitoes in space.

That left four.

A couple more mishaps occurred as we negotiated the asteroid belt.

## The Hard Stuff

The two junior pilots, Obanja and Chang, came to blows. Over a woman. I know, incredible in the circumstances. Nurse Maua Makemake turned out to be the object of both their affections.

You do get brawls on ships. Cooped up together for years, little irritations can grow into big feuds. Not often so early in a mission. The problem in this case was Obanja armed himself with a traditional Kenyan *panga.* Severed his rival's right hand, so he did. Blood splashed all over the gymnasium. Place smelled of ammonia and disinfectant for days. They put Chang's hand back on of course, but they never really got it working the way it did before. Anyway, that was him confined to sickbay for months.

Obanja never stood trial for the crime. Turns out Chang's enmity had been more subtle. A simple screwdriver had loosened the vacuum seal of Obanja's helmet. The tiny defect didn't get discovered until after the Kenyan asphyxiated during an emergency drill in the brig.

Then there were two.

Colonel Takanova, our captain, grew concerned and did everything she could to wrap us in cotton-wool. She even insisted we should never eat the same meals in the mess.

Just as well. This precaution ensured only Angie Todhunter succumbed to botulism as a result of defective packaging in a portion of scampi. It started with nausea and vomiting; then she developed double vision and dysphagia and her speech became slurred. Eventually she needed a ventilator just to stay alive.

Now, just where is this morbid history leading us, you ask? *We don 't like to upset you*, you say, *but we have had more fun listening to lectures on the mating habits of the Rigelian Fern Frog.*

Well the point is, then there was one.

Just one pilot to take the controls as we approached Jupiter and our first slingshot. Naturally, since I'd kept my alcoholism secret from the crew, my sponsor was already several astronomical units astern and I had no one aboard I could turn to.

The point being, you see, I'd never actually flown a slingshot before. I'd performed perfectly in computer simulations during training; I'd sat beside both Connie and Angie as co-pilot; I knew in theory how to handle every conceivable emergency. *But* your first time through a slingshot you're supposed to have experienced back-up. For me there would be no-one.

Of course, for your first outbound slingshot you're travelling quite slowly to begin with. If the pilot attrition had occurred later, the pressure would've been worse. The second one is tougher because you're going faster. You seldom get the planetary conjunction you'd need for three. Just as well. Although, in theory, a triple could make far more distant stars accessible to human travellers; every explorer who'd ever attempted it had either crashed or disappeared into uncharted space. After the fourth disaster, attempts at triples were prohibited.

Colonel Takanova sent for me as soon as Angie fell ill. When I arrived in her ready room she actually got up and shook hands with me; would you believe that now? She grasped my right hand firmly with hers and my forearm with her left.

"I have every confidence in you, Lieutenant." She patted a chair beside hers, inviting me to sit. I'd never been in her ready room. She would've had no reason to see me before. Sinking nervously into an armchair so soft I felt in danger of disappearing, I struggled to sit upright, intimidated just by the room.

It was part office, part lounge. A bank of computer screens occupied one side, an abstract sculpture on a coffee table the other. Two internal doors led, I guessed, to a bunk room and a bathroom for when she couldn't spare the time to use her suite down in the accommodation module. There was even a hint of lily-of-the-valley clinging to the textiles. In fact, her ready room had more comforts than my home.

We sat in the lounge section. The captain looked at ease. I don't suppose I did.

"At the rate we're losing pilots we aren't going to make it out of the solar system, let alone to Tau Ceti." She smiled reassuringly, as though she dealt with such problems every flight.

Takanova was not yet fifty but already commanding her third deep-space mission. Not a grey hair lurked among her blonde curls and very few worry lines etched her face. Meeting her brought the crisis home. She'd been impressive, important, distant, like the president. Now, she sat right in front of me. Her uniform was immaculately tailored, her figure toned and fit, hair sleek, manner calm.

"Since you're my only pilot, at least for the outward leg, I'm relieving you of all other duties. Oblige me by not engaging in any vigorous sports or anything else that might lead to injury. And stay away from sickbay. Don't risk infection by offering commiserations to Leandros or Todhunter."

I nodded, my throat dry. "Aye, Captain."

Men at that time, you'll remember, were confident there would always be a woman to make sure they didn't foul up. That was just the way things were. The natural way. How could I be stressed with Leandros and Todhunter there to do the worrying? I'd always been backup. Now, *I* was a man in charge. Nothing like that had ever happened before.

"And another thing. Apart from flying, you'll need to train some new pilots. Give me your three best names–anyone in the crew you think looks promising. Best if you take people who're starting from scratch. We've half a dozen who flunked out of flying school, but I've checked their records and you can take it from me they won't do."

"Aye, Captain."

That was it. Meeting over.

So, in addition to being royalty, I was to be O'Flaherty the Kingmaker. I had real responsibility for the first time and it felt heavy. You know how it is; you always think you want something until you actually get it.

Well, the other guys on board just volunteered or expressed their enthusiasm as you might expect. They didn't suppose for a minute they had much of a chance to be selected as a trainee. But then there were the women.

The women had no such inhibitions. Women did not approach the selection process with diffidence. They were used to getting what they wanted. And for the first time in my life, there were women who wanted something from me. No women had previously thought it worthwhile to engage in aggressive competition for Brendan O'Flaherty.

Lola Montez stood five-foot-one, an olive-skinned brunette with bright eyes, a slinky walk, and wandering hands. She did little in the way of small talk. I tried to make it a rule never to disagree with her. We'd been together for several weeks, which in those polyandrous days counted as a stable relationship. Don't imagine a relationship of equals; I got the feeling she kept a man because they wouldn't let her bring her dog on board.

Anyway, Lola held the post of deputy-chief navigator and a female boss blocked her way to further promotion. Naturally, being a woman and ambitious, she expected me to ease her way into Leandros' chair.

I knew a thing or two about Lola, and amongst the things I knew was she'd make a lousy pilot. You need to be adaptable, sensitive to the feel of your ship long before the instruments register a problem. I can't explain. It's something you either sense when you handle the controls or you don't.

Lola did everything by the book, at precisely the moment the book said to do it. Professionally, she lacked imagination. She was to sensitivity what an elephant is to etiquette.

Not that I ever intended to explain any of this to her. She had a couple of good points. My life would be easier, I reckoned, if she flunked pilot training of her own accord rather than having me tell her in advance.

Third Engineer Marika Söderström qualified as the archetypal blonde bombshell, six-foot-tall and statuesque. Her ancestors helped Leif Erickson discover America. The only thing Marika ever looked like discovering was the best place to hit a piece of recalcitrant machinery with a hammer. She lacked patience but she did not lack ambition.

Normally the third-string pilot would've been beneath her notice. I measured three inches shorter than her, among other things. However, since these were not normal times, Marika sent 'round her batman to invite me to dinner.

"I'm with Montez right now," I told him.

"And you're complaining because a couple of women want to fight over you?" he asked. "What can it hurt? In any case if I go back with 'no' for an answer she'll bite my head off–maybe literally."

"It's not *your* head I'm worried about!"

Nevertheless, we men used to be known for our willingness to take risks. I suppose a little of the reckless legacy of my bog-trotting, cattle-thieving, O'Flaherty ancestors still remained. With the whiff of danger in my nostrils, I told him I'd see Marika for dinner. Then I told Lola that on the captain's orders I had to interview other candidates and she shouldn't be upset.

"Hah! That muscle-brained weight-lifter!" she growled. Her dark eyes flashed and her accent became more pronounced, as it usually did when she became aroused. "She only got aboard because her mother's the District Commissioner for Europe. You can't take her seriously!"

"The captain wants three names." I had experience pouring oil on Lola's troubled waters. And elsewhere. "You want me to put forward two other names that *do* offer you serious competition?"

"Good thinking, *Burrito*," she exclaimed, her mood passing in an instant from thunder to sunshine. Her nickname for me meant little donkey not tortilla, though neither would have been very complimentary. "And who's the other lamb to the slaughter going to be?"

I told her I should really put forward a man for reasons of political correctness. The idea worried her even less than Söderström did. She'd counted her chickens before the eggs were even laid. I congratulated myself. That was about the last time I did anything right.

## The Hard Stuff

So, with a clear conscience I turned up for dinner that night. Marika had invited me to the French restaurant, a very pleasant small dining room on Deck Eight: individual latticed booths, an atmosphere redolent of garlic and a three-piece band playing old *chansons d'amour*. When you walk into the place you can feel yourself transported back into the Paris of several hundred years ago.

The staff costumes are modelled on the early twentieth century. They even simulate the look and smell of cigar smoke in the atmosphere. I'd never been there before; too expensive for my pay grade. This time Söderström would be picking up the tab. Out-of-uniform she scorned the usual coverall; she wore a dress–scarlet with silver trim. I found it hard to tell what held it together, what with the neckline plunging nearly to her waist and the three-foot slit up the side. If she wore anything underneath, it didn't show.

They say you should never judge a woman's state of mind by what she's wearing. Marika might be an exception. A vixen eyeing up a rabbit could hardly have made her thoughts more obvious.

She had legs that went on forever and scarcely fit under the small table. Long blonde hair, piled up on top of her head, made her look even taller. Her perfume might have been *Chanel* and her make-up might have been applied with a trowel. In view of her height rather than any antiquated notions of chivalry, she tactfully remained seated as I approached. This meant that, standing, I looked down on scenery that quite took my breath away.

Marika flashed an inviting glance from underneath inch-long false eyelashes. When I told her she looked stunning, she managed to flutter them. Even her eyelid muscles were finely toned. Granted, I might have preferred the whole package on a slightly smaller scale.

I let her advise me on the menu, hesitating to demur when she ordered a thirty-year-old bottle of *Chateau Yqem* that probably added a significant percentage to the public debt of Sweden. A little hiccup intruded in our relationship when she offered to pour and I told her I didn't drink. But her campaign couldn't be deflected by minor setbacks.

Well before coffee, her signals would have made clear to any male who was not actually unconscious what sort of additional inducements would attend my placing her name on the shortlist. Marika's moves made Lola seem subtle.

Now, I'm no saint and I don't know too many men who are. I'm definitely not the sort of man to find opportunity easy to pass up.

"I can see your potential," I told her, as she leaned across the table towards me. "But you know my problem. Montez can be seriously jealous; this is a long mission and I don't need the sort of trouble she'd make if I advised the captain you'd make a better pilot."

"I could beat that Spanish midget with one hand tied behind my back! And that's not all I can do with a rope. You come to my cabin and I'll show you. You just tell the captain who's best and let me take care of her."

Well now, you can't say I didn't warn her, can you? Suffice it to say, the rest of the evening was just one big revelation after another.

I know what you're thinking. *Just what exactly was your problem, Brendan, me old son?* But I'd been told to give the captain my top three names and all I did was name the first two women who asked me and one make-weight male. I couldn't nominate a talented male because I couldn't face having to tell the captain a man would make a better pilot than either of the women—and I don't mean the consequences from the captain.

That night the booze called to me louder than it had for a long time. Marika forgot I didn't drink and offered me whiskey when we got back to her cabin. *It might steady my nerves.* But what else might it steady? I remembered I was in AA. But nobody else in my locality was in AA, and therefore they wouldn't find out.

I know I should've stood up to the sexual bribery. Reprehensible weakness. But let me tell you, there's a hell of a lot of difference between dispassionate consideration for such a situation and actually being in it. A one-off opportunity. It had never happened before; it would never happen again, and any heterosexual male who says he'd have been able to stick by his principles has never seen the likes of Söderström naked, so he hasn't.

For the next few days I gave preliminary pilot training to both women, as well as my token male, and none of them made good. Neither of the women recognised their inadequacy, of course. As they saw it, if a man could be a pilot, then just how difficult could it be?

Remember, piloting a starship is not like piloting an aircraft. There's no atmosphere to provide resistance against which you can bank and turn. The thrust of your engines at any given time is tiny compared to the accumulated momentum of continuous acceleration. Even when you approach your destination, and you turn the ship around and run the engines against the direction of travel, you only achieve an extremely gradual deceleration. You rely on reverse slingshots for much of your braking.

## The Hard Stuff

The most important thing you do as a pilot is make thruster corrections that allow you to meet the next gravity field in the right plane and at the right angle of entry. Then, you adjust the attitude of your ship to emerge from said gravity field heading in the right direction for your encounter with the next one.

My male trainee honestly admitted he couldn't cope and gave up after two lessons. But it would've been against the order of nature, so it would, for a woman to admit inadequacy. Meanwhile each continued to use every available means to influence her trainer and sabotage her rival.

Because Jupiter is relatively easy *and* I already looked ahead to Uranus, I managed to go into the first slingshot still stone-cold sober and able to boast (albeit quietly and to myself) that I had not touched alcohol for over three years.

Both Montez and Söderström were allowed to sit beside me, but neither of them had much idea what they were watching, and as a result they passed the time trying to score points off each other. So, in addition to piloting, I had this background drama in which I played the part of a bone being fought over by two rival bitches. My powers of concentration wore thin.

"When do we reach light speed?" asked Söderström naively. I already suspected Lola was right about Marika's mother and her influence with the top brass.

"Idiot!" Lola exclaimed. "It's impossible to reach light speed. The closer you get to it the more fuel you need to burn per increment. Before you reach light speed you're losing more than you gain."

"Idiot yourself!" Marika flung back. "Tau Ceti is twelve light years from the solar system and we take two years to get there, which means we average six times light speed."

"*Burrito*, explain to her!" Lola placed her hands in her lap and sat back waiting for me to prove her right, since of course I had nothing better to do at the time.

"Technically, ladies, you're both right," I said, trying to keep the peace and concentrate on the approaching manoeuvre. "We don't achieve the speed of light but we do cover twelve light years in two Earth years, because all four dimensions, including time, are relative. The closer we approach light speed, the shorter a light year becomes relative to its length on Earth."

"Right!" nodded Lola, who had the brain to understand.

"I see," nodded Marika, who didn't.

Under the circumstances, we could consider ourselves lucky Jupiter is relatively easy. The slingshot went well enough, in fact it went great, but I was so wound up when I got back to my cabin I might well have fallen off the wagon there and then if I hadn't been forestalled.

It so happened I had the odd bottle of good whiskey stashed about the place, you see. Just a few. And a few more to be on the safe side. Then of course the never to be touched strategic reserve.

I made excuses to myself. Some days I would take out a bottle and look at it to remind myself how evil it was. Some days I didn't dare take it out. Days like this one.

Lola used the electronic key I'd given her.

"Olé!" she cheered. "I am the matador, no? And you, *Burrito*, would be good as picador if only you weren't trying so hard not to offend the stupid bull!"

"Her mother is the District Commissioner for Europe."

"You let me worry about that," she grinned lasciviously. "I have an idea."

I didn't ask. If she wanted me to know, she would've told me.

As it happened I guess she must have known Marika slept with someone. At the time she didn't suspect me, I think. One day in class the Swede acted unusually nervous and whispered an embarrassed admission she had missed a period.

Now, there's ordinary stress and then there's potential fatherhood, so there is. The issue had never even crossed my mind. I pointed out *I* was on the pill and it couldn't be my fault. Marika looked offended. Later Lola laughingly told me she'd spiked one of Marika's drinks with a hormone preparation.

Two days later, normal service resumed and Marika relaxed, but my poor reaction to the pregnancy scare made my name mud. I cast around for something to make the whole distasteful business go away and I hit upon the worst possible solution. Swearing her to total secrecy, I explained the cause of her problem.

The next day Lola's hair turned green and her skin turned orange. A fault in the plumbing of her cabin. An unattractively gaudy Lola demanded to know why I hadn't warned her. She bore a striking resemblance to a freshly scrubbed root vegetable with its leaves still attached and, to judge by the smell, the vegetable had until recently been well covered in horse manure.

"Be reasonable," I pleaded. "*You* didn't give *me* advance warning. Why do you suppose *she* would tell me anything?"

I could tell she wasn't convinced.

The pair of them went on like this, tit for tat so to speak, for several days. Marika's dress came completely apart one night at dinner and she had to flee from the restaurant clad only in a tablecloth.

Lola fell asleep whilst having her hairstyle restored and ended up with a crew cut.

Marika's uniform blouse shrank in the laundry and no replacements were available in her size.

Lola's uniform trousers disappeared altogether and she had to go on duty in shorts.

I was at my wits end and bitterly regretted what I'd gotten myself into. I looked so guilty, each of the women suspected I was a double agent. Meanwhile, my sponsor languished even more astronomical units astern.

The stress of remembering which woman was supposed to know what, doing my own calculations, *and* teaching at the same time became too much for my natural Irish fortitude. On the rare occasion they left me alone, I virtually climbed the walls, jumping at every little noise.

I expect most of you know the feeling. There's this combination of self-loathing and self-pity and there in the middle of it is you, on your own, when the person you really want to run away from is yourself. Anxiously, I checked all my calculations twenty times despite them coming out right every time. I wanted out of both relationships but I couldn't because both women were still determined to make pilot.

I was even fighting off *more* women who fancied their chances at taking over from the male drop-out. All I wanted was just five minute's privacy, anywhere. Hell, I would've got off the ship if there'd been anywhere to go.

In the absence of anyone I could talk to, in the end I resorted to the supposed comfort offered by a bottle. It's easily done. We *all* know how easily. I would only take one drink, you understand, just to steady my nerves. I could stop after one.

Then, after the first one I thought, *well, it wasn't a very large one; another won't do any harm.* You know how it goes. For five minutes or so I felt better. After that, I felt worse and needed another.

The next day I stumbled through class only semi-coherent and even Marika, who didn't often understand me when I was sober, could tell something was wrong. I had a worse problem the next day, and a dreadful one the day after that. The fourth day they scraped me off the floor of my cabin and carried me insensible to sickbay–*twelve hours* from our Uranus slingshot.

When I finally came to, I lay in one of the bright, white sickbay cubicles and about forty of my fellow countrymen, equipped with road drills, conducted excavations on my skull. My mouth contained a bloated piece of dry towelling that I eventually figured out was my tongue. I couldn't discern the distinction, if any, between up and down. Lying still felt like surfing.

Suddenly I was unbelievably nauseous. I threw up violently into a bucket held by someone beside the bed and lay back again thinking, *death has to be preferable to this*. Not, of course, that I had a great deal of grip on what exactly *this* was, except it involved consciousness. I had the nasty feeling if I remained conscious for much longer, I should have no choice but to resume awareness of something I'd rather not remember.

Then I heard a slight noise.

Despite the road drills, I opened an eye again. By concentrating very hard I blurrily focused on something that turned out to be a witness to my misery. A shape sat beside my bed.

I couldn't recognize my unwelcome visitor, but no-one should see me in this state. Perhaps with a superhuman effort I might be able to activate both my eyes and my voice simultaneously, and tell him or her to go away. I managed the eyes first and promptly wished I hadn't.

Colonel Takanova sat beside my bed. *She* held the bucket.

"So, Brendan, you're alive," she said softly.

"I might have to check on that and get back to you, Captain," I croaked. I needed help, but didn't have the wit to think who I was asking. "Is there any chance, do you suppose, a man could get a drink around here?"

She held a glass of water to my lips; it wasn't what I meant. The water reactivated the rancid taste of my saliva.

"It seems we have a little problem," she murmured.

I could just about cope with her whispering; if she'd spoken in a normal tone I might have passed out again.

"I know, Captain, I'm sorry," I slurred, trying to get my towelling tongue around the syllables and manoeuvre lips that felt like a new skin graft. "Give me five minutes, just, and I'll be ready for the Uranus pass."

In reality five hours, several gallons of black coffee and a prairie oyster *might* have had me just about ready to stand.

"Uranus was yesterday," she whispered. "I'm afraid it didn't go well."

"What?" I struggled to sit up. With an effort of will remarkable under the circumstances, I dislodged a dozen or so of the road menders. The captain supported my back and stuffed an extra pillow behind me. Then she held the water glass to my lips again and made me take another sip.

"When they couldn't bring you out of it I had to choose between aborting, which would've meant eighteen months just to get back to Earth, or letting your trainees handle the slingshot. Both of them swore they could do it. My mistake. I'm ashamed to admit, I'm usually inclined to take a woman's word whereas I sometimes wonder whether a man isn't just boasting."

"Neither of them could be trusted to steer a straight line." I groaned. The remaining road menders staged a work-in, protesting the dismissal of their erstwhile comrades.

"Now he tells me!" The captain somehow managed an exclamation without raising her voice. "I realise with hindsight I should just have chosen one of them. At the time, it seemed like a good idea to let them help each other. Unfortunately, they fell out and more or less fought over the controls. Montez wanted to rely mostly on the computer, but she hadn't much idea about the input data. When that seemed to go astray, Söderström hit the manual override and broke off much too early. As a result, we're not on course for Tau Ceti."

"Are we on course for anywhere?"

"Given the billions of possible destinations"–she smiled that reassuring smile of hers–"you're always on course for somewhere; the only questions usually are how long it'll take to get there and whether you're likely to be still alive by the time you arrive. In our case I suppose you might consider us lucky. We somehow stayed on the plane of the ecliptic."

"Coming off the ecliptic is slingshot lesson three," I said. "They're both still on lesson one."

"Which maybe makes me luckier than I deserve." She frowned. "But since we broke off too soon, we're headed back sun-wards. I'm not a pilot, but by my reckoning we're on a collision course for Jupiter. Since our speed is so high, we'll crash within forty-eight hours–unless you can use the Jovian gravity field for braking."

You can tell I wasn't my usual diffident self, or I never would've had the temerity to contradict *any* female superior, much less the captain. I fear, on this occasion, the technical side of my brain was a good deal more functional than the social.

"No crash. Don't have to brake," I grated, not sure in fact whether I could even reach the pilot's seat without whiskey. My piloting skills were still sufficiently online for me to remember all the emergency simulations I'd been put through. "Double slingshot."

"That's never been done."

"And no-one ever used Jupiter for first braking Earthbound," I wheezed.

"So, one way or another we set a precedent." The captain bit her lower lip pensively. A double slingshot 'round Jupiter would more than compensate for our inaccuracy around Uranus. The distance we'd doubled back would be nothing, relatively speaking. We'd end up with two and a half slingshots and make Tau Ceti early.

At this late stage, I thought it would be a good idea to offer some excuse for the state I was in. "If only I didn't feel so bad. I have this headache–maybe a migraine. Maybe I've picked up a virus or something."

Feeble. I knew it. I knew the captain knew it. Even so, the effort of talking left me collapsed and sweating on the pillows.

"I believe, Brendan O'Flaherty could handle a double slingshot if I could have *him* back and not the self-pitying hung-over drunk in this bed." These were her first harsh words.

"I'm sorry," I mumbled again.

"I don't need 'sorry', I need O'Flaherty," she snapped. "You're fortunate I went through your cabin myself. Montez found you on the floor. I collected fifty bottles of whiskey. Twelve of them were empty."

There went the last shred of hope for my career. I felt like throwing up again. "I'm not sure quite why that makes me fortunate," I groaned.

Without whiskey, I figured I couldn't get the nerve up to fly the double slingshot. We'd all be dead. But *with* whiskey I couldn't fly around Jupiter because I'd be paralytic. We'd still be dead. It was all too much for my poor brain.

"You're fortunate because I found something else in addition to the whiskey. I found a bronze medal for three years abstinence." The captain smiled wistfully.

"Ah, that! I'll have to return that," I sighed.

"I'll hold it for you. In three years' time, when we're half-way back from Tau Ceti, you can have it back–if you've earned it."

My half-drowned brain couldn't handle the information. "I don't get it.

You're going to trust me *again*? I'm an alcoholic. You trusted me and I let you down. I'm a waste of space even in space, where there's a lot of it. Why give me a second chance?"

"Everyone deserves a second chance," she answered quietly. "Most of us need it at some time or other. You didn't have a sponsor. You tried to cope on your own because you were ashamed. I understand that, but you know you can't do it on your own. You. Need. help. You need a friend."

"You mean …" In the first place my comprehension was still slow, and in the second place I couldn't believe my ears.

"I didn't think I'd ever say this to a man," the captain said. "I was surprised to find myself so sexually prejudiced. Not anymore. There are fifty of us on board, Brendan, and I'm going to be your sponsor, if you'll have me."

I couldn't find any words.

"Let me introduce myself formally," said my commanding officer. "My name is Olga Takanova and I am an alcoholic."

"Hello, Olga," I whispered.

"Hello, Brendan." She smiled.

Well friends, after that the captain herself sat beside me as we performed the second Jupiter slingshot. Just a few days earlier her being there would've destroyed my slender self-confidence. But instead, the nearness of my new sponsor helped mightily. She relied on me. She trusted me. Her faith helped me beat the craving.

I don't have to explain to you how it works. We've all been through it. This time I'm dried out for good. I'm more grateful to the captain than I can say, so I am.

In our small way, we made space flight history. The first starship *ever* to do more than two slingshots and survive. The first to do a double pass of Jupiter. Probably the last ever to perform a Jupiter pass at such a speed.

Maybe more important in the long run, we're the first starship with a male chief pilot and full sex equality on board. I'd like to think others will follow, so I would.

That's my testimony. I'm Brendan O'Flaherty. I'm an alcoholic. I've been sober for three years, and I'm proud to receive this bronze medal.

Born in Yorkshire, Oxford graduate Philip Brian Hall is a former diplomat and teacher. He has stood for parliament, sung solos in amateur operettas, rowed at Henley Royal Regatta, completed a 40 mile cross-country walk in under 12 hours and ridden in over one hundred horse-races over fences. He lives on a very small farm in Scotland with his wife, a dog, a cat and some horses.

Philip has had short stories published by (among others) AE The Canadian Science Fiction Review, Flame Tree Publishing (UK) and Cosmic Roots & Eldritch Shores (USA). His novel, 'The Prophets of Baal' is available as an e-book and in paperback.

# The Witch's Intern

by M. M. Pryor

My release from school lasted approximately one hour and thirty-eight minutes when my mother sat down at the kitchen table, pushed the spine of my Michael Crichton novel down far enough so she could see my eyes, and said, "Amelia, have you applied for any summer jobs yet?"

I removed the popsicle from my mouth, wiping my free hand at some syrupy drool running down my chin. "Jesus, Mom."

"Your dad and I just think that it'd be good to find something to keep busy. You'll head off to Stanford in the fall, and it'd be nice for you to save up a little nest egg for yourself. I don't want to put any pressure on you, but you never know what unexpected expenses you might have, and with your older brother in college, too, we can't really afford–"

"I know, I know. I'll get around to it, okay? Just give me a day. Jeez."

She shrugged, then stood up. "I've got to pick up your sister. Don't eat too much. We're going to have an early dinner."

She floated out of the kitchen as easily as she'd breezed in, leaving in her wake the Help Wanted section of the local newspaper. Man, my mother fought dirty. I had a compulsion to read any form of printed material in front of me: the back of cereal boxes at breakfast, fashion magazines in dentists' offices, newspapers, you name it.

I was in the middle of a boring passage in my book anyway, so I set it aside, then reached out and picked up the Help Wanted section. Smoothing the crease, I laid it flat on the kitchen table. Scanning the columns, I eliminated job after job I wasn't eligible for: anyone interested in roof repair or manual labor wouldn't hire a scrawny, not-quite-18-year-old girl, with a beat-up Honda Accord.

I circled a few ads I wasn't exactly *thrilled* about, but was at least eligible for: ice-cream server, dog walker, and bagger at the grocery store down the road. As I folded up the newspaper to set it aside, one last ad caught my eye. It was buried in the middle of the back page:

# M. M. Prior

WANTED: SUMMER INTERN. A'S IN BIOLOGY AND CHEMISTRY REQUIRED. IDEAL CANDIDATE GOOD WITH ANIMALS. SENSE OF DISCRETION REQUIRED. BRING REPORT CARD TO 37 WINTERASH LANE TO APPLY. PAID POSITION.

It was the weirdest ad I'd seen, but I circled it anyway. Though I leaned toward dog walker–I *did* like animals, especially dogs–and being outside sounded a lot better than being stuck indoors shoveling ice cream into crumbling cones or loaves of bread into plastic bags, but I might as well examine all my options, right?

Even though 37 Winterash Lane was only across town, my abysmal sense of direction required me to use Google Maps to find the specific street. As I slowly drove my car, one eye glued to the directions spooling out on my phone, the streets became more and more familiar until, I miraculously stumbled across the place. Set slightly back from the road, the house's original color could've been anything, but the paint had long ago faded to grey and started peeling like a bad sunburn. Many of the windows were boarded shut.

I'd been here before. Kids pranked each other all the time, especially around Halloween, to visit the creepy old witch who lived in the boarded-up house across town. When speaking about the house, no one used the address, simply called it *the Witch's house*, in the same reverent tone 11-year-old girls whisper Bloody Mary's name at sleepovers.

No one, as far as I knew, actually *saw* the occupant of 37 Winterash

Lane, so I'm not sure why or how the witch rumor spread; but one look at the house presented some pretty strong evidence in favor of its truth.

"Don't be ridiculous," I told myself. "Witches don't place Help Wanted ads. Just go up there and tell her you saw the ad and if she's terrifying, leave and go scoop ice cream for all the other kids in your year—whose parents *don't* force them to get jobs during their last summer before college, because they're not the worst parents ever."

After a few minutes of strategizing, I decided on a straightforward approach. Marching up to the door, I rang the bell.

No response.

I checked my watch. It was 11:13 a.m. Maybe whoever lived at 37 Winterash Lane was out running errands or brewing potions in the basement, or whatever witches do.

I weighed my options. I could leave, but what if the witch was already on her way to the door? If I left now, I'd still be jobless and I would've bothered her for no reason. If she really *was* a witch, I didn't want to risk getting cursed for annoying her.

Finally, the door creaked open. Against the utter darkness emanating from the bowels of the house, I could barely make out a thin, slumped shadow propped up on a cane.

"Yes?"

I stared at her. I wasn't sure what I thought the witch would look like, but the woman standing in front of me wore an immaculate white lab coat, and a pair of huge lens-glasses dangled from a lanyard around her neck. Not exactly witch-y garb. Where were the flickering lanterns and mouse bones tangled in her hair?

"Um …"

She raised one eyebrow.

As if someone had plugged my brain in, I finally remembered why I stood on this woman's porch.

"Your ad."

"My … ad."

"Yes." I nodded, shifting gears in my brain until it was up to speed again. "I'm checking to see if, um, the position is still available?"

She folded bony hands across her chest with yellow-stained fingertips.

I smiled wide and tried to look trustworthy. "I brought my report card."

As I reached into my bag to fetch the report card as proof, a giant shadow burst out of the front door, struck me in the stomach, and knocked me off my feet.

"Tiberius, you dumb mother–" The witch yelled at the beast. It whined, a wet, ear splitting whimper, and settled onto its back haunches. It was, I realized, how the dog sat; its forepaws were miserably short. A birth defect?

As I picked myself up off the porch, face inches away from Tiberius', I got a good look at the dog; which I instantly regretted. His skin stretched tightly over his body. Half of it shone greasy and a gross mold-colored peach fuzz covered the other half. The mongrel appeared to suffer from the most disgusting case of mange I ever saw.

"Nice, uh, nice … dog you have there. What type is he?"

The witch grabbed Tiberius' collar and tried to contain the energetic beast. Her lips squeezed tight; all I could think was I'd definitely blown any chance of getting the job.

"You're hired."

"What?"

"Do you want the job or not?"

"I mean, I do. I think I do, but … don't you want to know what my greatest strength is or what my biggest struggle has been?"

"I'm too busy for that nonsense. If you want the job, I'll give you a shot. Trial basis. Last chance."

She started dragging Tiberius back into the house, leaving the door wide open. I tried to peer inside, but steeped as it was in darkness, I couldn't make anything out.

I felt like someone had tossed a coin and told me to call a side. In my mind, the coin tumbled through the air in slow motion, oscillating between my options. Heads: I could leave and spend the rest of my summer scooping ice cream and wondering what this woman needed an intern for; tails: I could follow her into the house and find out firsthand. I wasn't sure what would happen if I did, but I'd either get a good story, a job, or both.

I stepped inside.

Shadows bathed every nook and cranny in the house. My eyes adjusted as we made our way down the hall. A bookcase loomed at the end, covered with elegant leather-bound tomes. When the witch reached out to touch one of the books, I felt my lungs stop, expectation heavier than oxygen.

One of her fingers tipped a particularly thick volume out of its place on the shelf and a mechanical click echoed from inside the wall.

I had to cover my mouth to keep her from seeing my grin. *A secret passage behind a bookcase!* I had a lifelong obsession with genre fiction: science fiction, fantasy, mystery, anything. I was part of a generation who'd grown up waiting for a letter from Hogwarts, who would've traded anything to join Starfleet or travel to the bottom of the sea in the *Nautilus.*

The corner of her mouth lifted, and I felt a pang of embarrassment when I realized her amusement at my reaction.

As the bookcase swung away from the wall, I saw not a passage, but the top of a spiral staircase. Tiberius pulled away and ran down the rest of the steps. I trailed after them. A moment later a *thud* shook the risers beneath me.

We sped down the last few steps, and when we turned the corner, I saw Tiberius sulking near a thick, glass door with a keypad next to it.

"He does this all the time," she said.

I barely heard her, too busy gawking at the secret laboratory set up in the basement of 37 Winterash Lane. That was, after all, the only explanation for what I was staring at. Behind the glass door–one of those impeccably clean sliding glass doors all the high-tech government labs use in movies–were rows and rows of counters crammed with cages. Inside the cages were tiny colorful creatures. I couldn't make out what they were, but I felt certain about one thing–this woman standing next to me was my Gandalf. My Dumbledore. She was the key to my very own adventure.

"Who *are* you?" I asked.

"My name is Ursa Black."

I'd never head of her, of course. No one in the world had. At least not yet.

"Yeah, but what are you *doing* down here?"

"Genetically engineering dinosaurs," she said as simply as another eighty-year-old woman might have said "baking pies" or "watering my petunias."

"Shut the front door."

Ursa frowned. "It is shut."

I shook my head. "No. I mean, are you *serious*? About the dinosaurs?"

"Yes. Tiberius is half-Tyrannosaurus Rex and half-Pitbull."

"And you need an intern? Why? You look like you've been doing this by yourself just fine."

"Things change."

She didn't seem inclined to elaborate. It didn't matter. I had a whole summer to ask her all the questions bubbling up under my skin.

"I'll take the job!"

After the first few weeks, each shift progressed in the same pattern. Immediately after clocking in, I'd check the logs. Ursa often left me messages, changes in the creatures' diets, and progress updates about new batches of hatchlings. The logs were a recent development.

During the brief trial basis of my quasi-internship, Ursa never left the lab. But one day, a couple shifts after she told me I could keep coming around if I wanted, she needed to step out for a few minutes. That was the first time she left me alone and in charge of the lab.

Whenever Ursa said she was "stepping out," she didn't actually go anywhere. She just headed into a separately sealed off room at the other end of the lab. It had a different set of security measures than the main lab. Ursa would disappear and reappear at whim; sometimes she'd be gone for a few minutes, other times I wouldn't see her for weeks. I itched to ask about her absences, but even though Ursa trusted me to feed her experiments, her confidence in me stopped at the fingerprint reader screwed into the wall next to the mystery door.

Ursa never talked about what was inside that lab, or what she did there, or even in fact referred to it, except in the context of "stepping out." In my head, I called it the Secret *Secret* Laboratory of Ursa Black, and as the days crept by, I became more than a little obsessed with the mysteries contained behind that door. Sometimes at night, right before I went to bed, I made up stories about what was in the Secret *Secret* Laboratory. Maybe Ursa was a female Bluebeard and had hidden away a series of murdered grooms.

When my parents asked about my job, I lied and said I was filing claims for the local veterinary's office. We didn't have any pets, so no risk of my parents dropping by to visit me. Plus, it was the most boring thing I could think of, which, I hoped, would prevent them from showing too much interest.

I lied because I promised to keep Ursa's secret, but it was more than that. Ursa and her lab were the coolest things that ever happened to me, and I didn't want to share them with anyone.

But as the weeks flew by and Ursa spent more and more time in the sealed off part of the basement laboratory, I wished I could talk to someone about her behavior.

Sometimes when I showed up, Tiberius' bowl had been licked clean. This time, however, I couldn't locate any extra bags of food stashed away. Tiberius kept looking at me with his unblinking eyes. I fed him half the tuna sandwich I brought as I waited for Ursa to emerge. Hours slipped by, but she didn't appear.

I wanted to stay, but I had to go home. I couldn't afford to be late to dinner in case my parents called for me at the veterinarian's office.

I tried to check in with Ursa before I left, but the fingerprint checkpoint buzzed red at me, so I fed Tiberius the other half of the sandwich and wrote a note.

That night, I poked at dinner until my mother lifted her eyebrows and started to ask, in that inconvenient motherly way she had, if I was alright.

"Just feeling under the weather. Think I'll go to bed."

I carried my full plate into the kitchen, but instead of scraping it into the garbage, I dumped the contents into a plastic container and stuck it in the fridge, behind the orange juice. If Ursa didn't receive my note, Tiberius would need the food, at least until I figured out Ursa's Amazon Prime password so I could re-order his specialty kibble.

The next morning, I grabbed my leftovers. They seemed a meager offering, so I loaded my backpack with the rest of the deli meat, a bunch of bananas, and a jar of peanut butter before I headed over to Ursa's.

After the last security door whooshed open and I had a clear view of the desk, I saw my note hadn't been disturbed. I felt a chill settle over my skin.

"It's just the A.C.," I told myself, even though no amount of cold could cut through all the heating lamps set up in the basement.

Tiberius lay curled up under the desk. Upon my arrival, he loped out of his hiding place and knocked his gigantic head against my knee. I rubbed the already-forming bruise and shook my head.

"What do we do, buddy?"

Tiberius glanced at the fingerprint scanner mournfully.

"I don't think we're supposed to bother her," I told him while emptying the leftovers into his bowl. I put the deli meat in the cold storage and the rest of the food on the desk.

After a few failed attempts to concentrate on my work, which resulted in mixing up the data I collected from a group of miniature flying squirrel-pterodactyl hybrids, I gave up. I stalked over to the fingerprint reader and stared at it for a moment before scanning my hand again. It lit up red. UNKNOWN.

"*Damn* it, Ursa. Tiberius needs you."

At the sound of his name, Tiberius knocked into me again, forcing my hand against the scanner. It lit up red, but instead of saying UNKNOWN, the screen asked, ENGAGE EMERGENCY PROCEDURE?

I glanced at Tiberius. "Your call, buddy."

Tiberius' tongue lolled out of his mouth and he stared at me with a new quality of desperation. I hit the button.

An alarm blared. After the longest five seconds of my life, the screen said MANUAL EMERGENCY PROCEDURE ENGAGED. I pushed the door open and stepped inside the Secret *Secret* Laboratory.

Cold fell over me. The basement was warm, because of all the eggs. Compared to it, the sealed off part of the laboratory was freezing. Shivering, I made my way into the room. Light blinded me. Rows and rows of fluorescent lights hung from the ceiling. Running parallel to the lights sat trenches of dirt, from which sprouted green plants with mustard-colored centers.

"Ursa? Sorry for barging in like this, but Tiberius is–"

I stopped talking when I saw her. It took me a minute to pick her out as she lay hidden in the very back of the room, stretched on a cot. Tiberius and I scrambled to her side. One look at her and I knew she wasn't well. Feverish, despite the cold.

"What happened?"

"Time."

"It's, like, 9:15 a.m. Let me check–"

Ursa gripped my wrist with weak fingers. "No, I'm running out of time." She gestured to the rest of the room, the plants. "*Rhodiola rosea.* Native to my land."

"What does it do?"

"Extends life."

"You're kidding, right?" I asked, even though I knew Ursa never joked.

"I failed."

"I'm sure you can try again. It's not too late. Look, I'll help–"

Ursa shook her head. "When I was thirteen years old I was recruited to Stanford University. It was 1906."

I did the math in my head. She would've been 93 by the time I was born, and 110 that day. Impossible. She was old, of course, but there was no way a 110-year-old lived alone and worked full-time in her basement laboratory.

"You need a doctor."

"Doctors, *pwah*. No. A doctor will tell me I'm dying."

"But–"

"Listen. I was a doctoral candidate, but I never had the chance to defend my dissertation. The earthquake leveled the school. *Not* my fault. But everyone was so full of superstition back then, they thought I was Siberian witch. No one would hire me. I've spent my lifetime working alone. Working on these experiments. But now I must change focus. Take care of Tiberius. Continue the experiments. Don't disturb me. I just need time."

I didn't know how to break it to Ursa, but I wasn't sure she *had* time. Still, I did as she said. Before I shut the door behind me, I asked Ursa about Tiberius' food.

I thought I would feel better once Tiberius ate, but I didn't. Previously, I'd been oblivious to the enormity of what lay hidden behind that door and now I didn't know what to do about it. Since I'd hidden all of this from everyone in my life, I didn't have anyone to talk to, and even if I did, what would I say?

Ursa was dying. Even if the root worked, even if she could grow a good batch in time, she was 110. How much longer could she prolong the inevitable?

I sunk into a routine. Every day I went to the lab, fed Tiberius, and checked on Ursa's experiments. I never saw her, of course. She'd reengaged the security measures on the Secret *Secret* Laboratory and I took it as a hint she wanted to be left alone.

Ursa was still alive, because occasionally things would be different about the lab. Food would disappear or trash would appear, neatly tied in a black garbage bag. I tidied up after Ursa and stocked the fridge.

When summer drew to a close, I made a decision. I didn't ask my parents, but wrote to Stanford and delayed my enrollment. Stanford would always be there. This–what I was doing in Ursa's basement–was a once-in-a-lifetime opportunity. At least that's what I told myself. In reality, I didn't know what to do. If I left, who'd take care of Ursa? Tiberius? The experiments?

Finally, nine months into my gap year, Ursa emerged. She looked younger than before; *much* younger. And for the first time, I was struck by the similarities between us. Our skin had the same shade of light brown. Her hair, once white, now gleamed as dark as mine.

I'd waited so long for that moment, had thought of a million things to say. But once I was actually confronted with it, I realized I only had one option.

I'd done a lot of thinking over the last several months. If the earthquake hadn't happened, if the rumors hadn't gotten out of control, if she'd had the support of her professors, who knows what kind of scientific developments our world might have seen in the last century?

I dug my Stanford welcome packet out of my backpack and held it out to Ursa.

"They'll never know the difference."

Ursa smiled at me, a full, genuine, happy smile, and tears ran down her cheeks. She shook her head. "No, child."

"Take it," I insisted. "You deserve a second chance."

"I've already been given one. Now, I want to see the sun."

As Ursa went upstairs, I fed the creatures, swept the lab, and I eyed the cages which needed changing. Finally, I couldn't stand it. I ran up to the main floor and checked all the rooms, the back yard, and the front yard. Everywhere.

Ursa Black had vanished.

When I returned to the lab, I noticed Ursa had disabled the security system on the Secret *Secret* Lab. All of the plants were ripped up. The massacred foliage lay covered in icy particles. That's when I understood.

Ursa had already given a lifetime of science to a world that hadn't wanted her. How could I ask her to give more?

Returning to the lab, I shredded the papers, erased the computer, and after a long debate with myself, decided to drop off the less suspicious creatures at the no-kill shelter in the next town over. The others I drove to the woods and released. I couldn't bring myself to euthanize them.

Then I packed a bag, slipped the welcome packet into the top of my suitcase, and whistled for Tiberius. He hopped up into the passenger seat of my car.

"Ready for Stanford, boy?"

My summer job had come to an end. It was time for me to carve out my own path. I was no longer Ursa's intern. No longer the shadow of a woman who had been ahead of her time. Ursa had been given a second chance. Who knew what she would do with it? Who knew what I would do with mine?

Tiberius just grinned, his tongue lolling out of his mouth over the rows of sharp teeth.

"Atta boy."

M. M. Pryor graduated from Vermont College of Fine Arts with an M.F.A. in Fiction in 2014. Since Starfleet doesn't exist yet and pterodactyl rider stopped being a viable occupation about 65 million years ago, M. M. settled for drinking a lot of coffee and writing tiny stories in the beautiful Pacific Northwest. M. M.'s short stories have been produced as podcasts and published in literary magazines, such as Gertrude and PANK. M. M. is currently at work on her first novel, a love story about a ghost. More of her work can be viewed on her website, mmpryor.com.

# Hunting Ground

by M.C. Tuggle

My visitor didn't leave my office until after midnight. He'd promised information that would clear my client of murder; but after hearing him out, I was too shaken to ask questions or even to thank him. I recall mumbling good bye and staring at him as he walked out the door.

When I gripped the doorknob, my hand trembled. What he'd told me couldn't be true, yet the man's explanation of how Donald Wyatt died not only fit every known fact of the case, but also with facts only I and my investigator knew. Plus, the local farmer told his story so convincingly I could swear he thought it was the truth.

And I could always spot a liar. It's my business.

I sank into my chair and re-read my notes on his statement. By 2:30 AM I had a plan: *modify* the farmer's unbelievable story just enough to build a defense for my client, Ryke Jeffries. But to do that, I'd have to interview a couple of potentially hostile witnesses and hope they'd tell me what I needed to know. It was my client's only chance.

The next afternoon, I drove to the old Kearns Farm, a vacant rural property between High Point and Greensboro. Once the model of a prosperous North Carolina tobacco farm, it had been in the center of legal battles for over fifteen years.

I got out of my car and looked around. Weeds and saplings choked its fields, and shattered limbs from tall pecan trees littered the yard—torn from their trunks by last winter's ice storm. The white, two-story farmhouse sagged at the roofline, and the slats in the front porch had faded and warped. A rusted screen door dangled on one hinge.

Perfect spot for a murder scene. Even the optics worked against my client. Add that to his boneheaded threats on local television and, well, I had my work cut out for me.

I turned toward the sound of tires scraping to a stop in the gravel driveway and saw the man I'd come to meet. He slid out of his red Toyota pickup and bounded toward me.

"Good morning. I'm Buddy Vuncannon. I appreciate you coming out here, Trevor."

He pumped my outstretched hand. "Glad to help, Mr. Vuncannon."

"Call me Buddy."

He stooped a bit and pointed behind me. "Look at the deer beside that old log barn!"

I glanced at the deer out of politeness, but returned my gaze to Trevor Tandem. He behaved exactly the way I'd expected after our brief phone conversation, and from reviewing his resume.

It was a warm June day, but Trevor wore a long-sleeved flannel shirt. The man was tall and skinny, and the tight, straight-leg jeans he wore magnified the effect. A black-and-teal Carolina Panthers cap sat on his head with the bill forward, causing tangles of brown hair to poke out.

"Yeah," I said. "Pretty. I appreciate you coming out here. Let's walk down to where Wyatt was found."

"Sure."

Trevor took long, effortless strides down the overgrown trail. I'm a jogger and had a hard time keeping up.

"Trevor, as I said on the phone, I'm defending Mr. Ryke Jeffries."

"Uh-huh."

I walked faster and leaned forward to get a better look at his face. "How long have you worked for Carolina Drilling?"

"Let's see—oh, about eight months."

"How did you get your job as a site evaluator?"

Still at full stride, he turned and said, "My dad knew the owner."

Nothing evasive about that response. And those round blue eyes radiated simple truthfulness. It's always a good idea to ask questions you already know the answers to. That gives a good baseline for when you really start to probe.

"So, in your capacity working for Carolina Drilling, you first check out a potential site to make sure your operations won't be a threat to the water supply?"

With a broad smile, Trevor said, "That's me."

"And you approved it?"

"Oh, sure. No problem."

"And Mr. Wyatt, the victim, came out here after you finished your report to determine the equipment needed for drilling?"

"Yep."

Before I could ask my next question, I heard something behind us. I stopped and stared into the brushy path. Barely audible over the chirps of birds and the rasping of cicadas, I heard rhythmic scrapes of hard leather on sandy soil. Someone hurried toward us. "Hold on, Trevor."

Moments later, a large, round man emerged from behind a bush in the trail. He wore a short-sleeved white shirt without a tie, billowing khaki pants, and dusty but new black shoes. His hair was also black, too black for the wrinkled forehead and drooping jowls.

He fixed me with a bulldog stare. "Oh, Vuncannon. Glad I found you. Dathan Robinson. I'm with Carolina Drilling."

I nodded. "Mr. Robinson."

He held out his hand. "Dathan, please." I let him grab my hand and he grinned while giving it a good mauling. "Okay if I call you Buddy?"

"Sure, Dathan." It was all I could do to hide my pain.

Robinson craned his head over my shoulder. "Good morning, Trevor."

"Hey, Mr. Robinson."

Robinson faced me. "My secretary told me you'd asked Trevor to come out here. Figured I'd join you and see if I could help in any way."

I gave him a closed-mouth smile. "Glad to hear that. We were headed for the location where they found Wyatt."

"Lead on."

We continued walking down the footpath toward the marsh. More water-loving alder trees appeared, and the sharp smell of soggy bottomland wafted our way. I looked back to see Trevor striding directly behind me, a wide grin on his face. Dathan Robinson dodged a branch Trevor let snap back, and mumbled under his breath.

This was a complication I didn't need. Robinson owned Carolina Drilling, the company that had leased the mineral rights to the Kearns Farm after a protracted court battle. My client, Rykee Jeffries, was an environmental activist, and had confronted Robinson about his company's plans to extract natural gas by fracking. No doubt, Robinson had raced here to make sure his employee cooperated fully. No doubt.

Robinson's nose and forehead puckered as he wiped a spider web off his face. "So, Buddy, what were you looking for here? We're ready to start operations."

"I have a few loose ends to nail down. I was about to ask Trevor if he saw anything unusual about the land when he conducted his groundwater impact study."

Dathan didn't skip a beat. "You mean like other booby traps? Like the one that killed Wyatt?"

I stopped and frowned at Dathan. "That's part of my problem. I had a guy who was a Ranger in Afghanistan look at the scene. He knows all about traps. But he tells me there's no sign of a trap that could open up and bury a man. Not where Wyatt's body was found, or anywhere else in the area."

"Hell, Vuncannon, what's the point of stomping around out here with spiders and snakes? You've seen the reports. It was in the news. Jeffries' terrorist friends covered up the evidence."

I pressed on down the trail. "When I was in law school, I had a professor who used to say, 'The landscape has stories to tell, and every room in every house bears witness to countless crimes.' In other words, you can study reports, review old court cases all you want, but there's nothing like looking around at the actual scene."

Robinson responded with a grunt. We kept walking.

In less than a minute, we reached the spot where they'd dug up Donald Wyatt. It was situated beside a small bog, a narrow strip of acrid water dotted with tiny islands covered in sedge. The pungent, earthy smell of the bog hovered in the air, almost as thick as the mosquitoes. It was the first time I'd visited the scene. To our left, just as the old farmer had told me last night, was the concrete block pig house. Waist-high and gray, it had a solidness about it despite the years. And a strange silence, too, exactly like the old farmer described.

Dathan and I stopped, but Trevor kept going. He twisted halfway around and said, "I'm gonna check something." Long arms waving for balance, he treaded his way on clumps of quaking earth.

Dathan shook his head. "Guess he isn't afraid of snakes."

I pointed to a flat stretch of sandy soil between us and the bog. "That's where the cadaver dog found Wyatt's body. Thing is, there's no sign a hole was dug here."

"Yeah, I saw it on TV. Jeffries' wacko terrorist friends covered it up."

"Thing is, two deputies stood watch near the old farmhouse that night, and didn't hear or see a thing. Plus, there were no footprints, no tire tracks, nothing. No evidence anyone tampered with the crime scene."

Dathan glowered at me. "I can understand you want your client to get a fair trial. But Mr. Jeffries made threats against me and my people. Said he was gonna keep us from drilling one way or another."

"I understand that. So, the sooner I can get what I need, the better." I nodded at Trevor, who was squatting on a shaky piece of ground in the bog. He looked ecstatic. "Trevor seems to love his work."

"That he does."

"Interesting background. He dropped out of five different programs in four different colleges. Then Carolina Drilling agreed to hire a groundwater impact expert as part of your court settlement. The deal was no fracking until the area had been inspected and approved."

A long, falling whistle came from the bog, and Dathan and I turned toward Trevor, who stood and shook his head. He started tip-toeing over the floating mounds.

"Yeah," said Dathan. "And that's what we did."

"How many sites has Trevor investigated and approved for you?"

Dathan faced me. His eyebrows formed thick black arches. "You know how many sites he's worked for us. Five. And yes, his opinion in each case was that local groundwater would not be affected by hydrofracking."

I smiled. "Who would've guessed?"

"Whoa!"

The sudden shout made me wheel toward the bog in time to see Trevor prance away from a large clump of tall weeds.

He pointed. "Copperhead! Big one."

Dathan leaned close to my face. "Look, Buddy. We agreed to hire a credentialed expert, and Trevor has a degree. He's also taken courses in geotechnical engineering."

"I know. He has a Bachelor of Science in general biology. And he's taken courses in just about everything."

"What's your problem with Trevor?"

Trevor jogged toward us, his wide, toothy grin undiminished by his run-in with the snake. He held something in his hand.

"Actually, I like Trevor. I just wonder about his ability to focus."

Catching Dathan's gaze, I added, "Of course, that could be an asset in certain situations."

Dathan swiveled his head toward me. His jaw tightened.

I smiled back, then turned. "You okay, Trevor?"

"Oh, yeah. I think I scared 'im more'n he scared me."

Dathan squinted at his employee. "What do you have there, Trevor?"

Trevor offered me and Dathan a closer look at the object in his hand. "Oh, this. It's a pH meter. I just took another sample. Bogs tend to be acidic, but this one shows levels I've never seen before."

Acidic? I bent for a closer look. "Is that unusual?"

"Yeah. Unreal."

That reminded me of an item I'd read in the Medical Examiner's report. "Could that explain the body's advanced state of decomposition? The ME's report said it looked like it had been eaten by acid."

Trevor's face wrinkled in a deep frown. "Oh, no."

"You're positive?"

Trevor raised a foot and grinned. The sharp stench of muck filled the air. "I stepped into that water when I ran from the snake."

That didn't help my client's case at all. But Trevor's knowledge of the area still might help me build a defense.

"I was wondering, Trevor, did you notice any sign of unstable soil when you tested this site?"

Dathan stepped between us. "Oh, I see where you're going with this. You think you can make the courts believe the soil's unstable so your client can stop us from drilling. Well, it isn't going to work."

In my best officer of the court voice, I said, "Dathan, you said you wanted to cooperate. Is it okay if your employee answers my questions?"

Dathan hissed, then nodded.

"What about it, Trevor? Any signs of unstable soil?"

Trevor glanced at the sky and was quiet a moment. Then he shook his head. "No. It's good Type B soil. Very stable."

"Quicksand, maybe, around the bog?"

"Oh, no. One of the things I check for is a confined aquifer. And there was no–"

"Wait, what? Can you explain?"

"If a flowing aquifer is confined by shale, it's under pressure. You don't want that near the drill site, 'cause that might affect drinking water in the area. Quicksand isn't like what you see in movies. There has to be moving water underground. There's no sign of that here."

Dathan heaved his bulk in between us again, but this time he bumped hard against my shoulder in the process. I gritted my teeth.

"See, Buddy? I told you Trevor here knows his job."

The sight of that jowly smirk just about did it. I felt my forehead radiate heat. Never had I been so tempted to throw the first punch.

But Dathan's comment made Trevor wriggle like a puppy getting his belly scratched. Seeing him helped me tamp down my temper. I had a job to do.

"Here's my problem, Trevor. Wyatt died of asphyxiation. His hands were not bound in any way, and there was significant blunt force trauma. That's consistent with being buried alive under unstable topsoil. But there was no sign of a booby trap. Any idea what could cause that?"

Trevor scrunched his forehead and stared into empty space. Then he cocked his head at me. "You know, that reminds me of the Mount Baldy Dunes on Lake Michigan. They call them the 'Living Dunes' 'cause they can suddenly open up and swallow people."

It took a few moments for that to register. All I could do was stare at Trevor. He'd echoed the same strange tale the old farmer had told me last night, and, despite the heat, I felt a cold shiver creep up my spine.

I took a long breath and said, "Swallow?"

"Yep. And scientists can't explain it."

"Look, Buddy," said Dathan. "Your client made threats on TV against my company. He and his environmental terrorist friends are behind this."

I nodded. "I know what Ryke said. But he's never committed a violent act in his life."

"Until now."

"We'll see." I looked at Trevor. "Anything else unusual about the area?"

He shook his head. "It's pretty typical for a peat bog. Low nitrogen levels, high pH, and the water's held in place by clay and granite. Flora and fauna–well, just about what you'd expect." Trevor shrugged in a way that suggested he sensed I was disappointed in his answer.

There were no more questions to ask. To defend Ryke Jeffries in court, I'd have to concoct quite a story and do a lot of table pounding. At least I'd learned certain land forms could suddenly and unexpectedly become unstable. That's all I had to work with to explain what happened to Donald Wyatt.

On the bright side, the prosecution had no witnesses, no DNA evidence, nothing to tie my client to the scene. What they did have was a threat, motive, and opportunity.

Dathan shuffled beside Trevor and gave him a fatherly clap him on the shoulder. He turned toward me, his face glowing in triumph. "We through here, Buddy?"

I couldn't stand that smirk, and turned what would have been a white-hot gaze toward the vacant pig house. "Yes." I turned back and said, "I suppose so. But Trevor, what'd you mean about the flora and fauna? You said it was *just about* what you'd expect."

"To be honest with you, I was a little disappointed. I'd a figured there'd be waterwheels in the bog. Or something like that."

Dathan and I turned and stared.

"Waterwheels?"

Trevor's eyes widened. "Yeah, they're plants that capture prey. Shrimp, tadpoles, even fish. They're related to the Venus Fly Trap, like we have on the coast."

That rekindled something the old farmer told me last night, and it made my chest tighten. "Why would you expect to find that here?"

"Because of the high pH levels in the water. You often see that associated with carnivorous plants."

It took a while for me to comprehend Trevor's analysis. As the implications became clear, I felt increasingly lightheaded. Trevor might just as well have hit me in the chest with a mallet.

One of the things the farmer said was old man Kearns, the previous owner, never could figure out who stole his pigs. Every few months, one would simply vanish without a trace. The farmer swore he'd seen his neighbor's pigs swallowed up by what he called "the hungry earth". Twice. I was the only soul he'd mentioned this to. No wonder.

Trevor frowned at me. "You okay, Mr. Vuncannon?"

"I'm fine. Just thinking." I stared at the spot where Wyatt had been buried alive. Just to be on the safe side, I backed away a few feet. "Trevor, let's imagine something. Just to explore an idea."

Trevor nodded energetically. "Okay."

"Now what?" Dathan wiped his forehead and folded both arms across his chest.

"It's just a little thought experiment. Trevor, is it possible for a section of soil to become alive?"

The big grin dissolved into a studious frown. "Are you serious?"

"You said certain plants became carnivorous because of the high acid content of the water in their environment. Could a section of the earth take on living processes? And somehow capture nutrients to feed those processes?"

Trevor whistled and shook his head. "I don't know about that."

"But if it did–might it perceive a threat to its life? And maybe protect itself the only way it could?"

Dathan rolled his eyes. "Okay, Buddy, I have no problem helping you defend your client. But now you're just wasting my employee's time. And mine." He spun around toward the footpath.

He stopped and stared past me. "Trevor, we're finished here. We have work to do."

"Yes, sir." Trevor's long legs carried him past me and Dathan and he strode away up the footpath.

Dathan swatted at a dragonfly. "Nasty swamp is all it is. I want to see our drills out here by the end of the week." He shot a sideways glance at me, and turned to follow Trevor.

At that moment, I saw Dathan Robinson stumble and fall to his knees in front of me. When I could comprehend what just happened, I froze. Dathan was waist-deep in swirling dirt.

"Get me out!" he screamed, arms flailing.

I stepped forward to grab his hand, but the ground collapsed under my foot. Somehow, I sprang back before toppling in.

Dathan's eyes glowed in terror. Then a shard of granite spiraled through the rotating dirt toward him and ripped into his arm. Dathan bellowed in pain. I risked another step closer. Then another.

Stretching out, I managed to reach him and clutched his bleeding arm in both hands. I leaned back, and pulled for all I was worth. The churning soil moved like cement turning in a mixer; I felt it sucking Dathan away from me.

I slipped forward. "Trevor!"

My heart throbbed from the effort, and the tortured muscles in my forearms burned. I shifted my weight and pulled until my shoulders threatened to pop out of their sockets. Dathan's head vanished under the roiling dirt.

I looked down. A wide crack stretched along a huge chunk of red clay under my feet.

Something grabbed my stomach, the pressure brutal. I was caught in a bear hug so tight it felt like my guts were being squeezed out.

"I got you, Mr. Vuncannon."

I wanted to tell Trevor to pull me by the chest instead of my stomach, but I couldn't breathe. Then I saw Dathan's head bob to the surface. He sputtered and gasped. His shoulders and chest appeared. Trevor jerked and Dathan slid out of the hole, belly-flopping onto the dirt.

Exhausted and aching, I dropped to my knees. Dathan and I lay on the ground, gasping for air.

When I looked up, Trevor stood over me. "What was that?"

It took me three labored breaths of air to regain my voice. "That, Trevor, is what I would call unstable topsoil."

Trevor's hand shot up, pointing toward the ground beside Dathan. "Look."

Despite my aches, I twisted my head and shoulders around. The sandy topsoil looked completely undisturbed.

It was the first time in my legal career when a development in one case helped me win another. The assistant district attorney dropped the murder charges against Ryke Jeffries, and Jeffries hired me to stop Carolina Drilling from hydrofracking natural gas on the old Kearns Farm. That case also never made it to trial, since Dathan Robinson finally agreed not to drill.

So, I guess I've boosted my status as an attorney. But if the *whole* story got out, my colleagues would call me crazy. They'd have a good case, too. After all, I believe Donald Wyatt's ability to focus on the task at hand is what got him killed, just as Trevor Tandem's inability to focus protected him.

And they'd really be convinced I was off my rocker if they knew what I think saved me and Dathan. No, it wasn't Trevor. It was the promise I made over and over in my head as I held tight to Dathan Robinson. *Release him, and I'll stop him from harming you.*

## Hunting Ground

It held up its end of the bargain. And I held up mine. One thing's for sure–I'll never look at open land the same way again.

M. C. Tuggle is a writer in Charlotte, North Carolina. His fantasy, sci-fi, and literary stories have appeared in several publications, including Aurora Wolf, The Flash Fiction Press, Space Squid, and Kzine. The Novel Fox released the paperback version of his novella Aztec Midnight in March, 2016. He blogs on literary topics at mctuggle.com.

# MOUNTAINS TO CROSS

By KT Wagner

Flakes of rust fly off the hacksaw blade as Mother works to remove the porcine yoke from my neck.

"Shut your eyes," she mutters. Her pregnant belly presses against my arm. The baby kicks and I pull away. The creases in Mother's face glisten and twist around her scowl. "You can't steer, if you can't see."

We waited almost two years for the temperature to drop low enough, and now we face a new enemy–time. My insides squirm in anticipation. I can't wait to leave and never return.

I'm my mother's fourteenth child and the first to survive past sixteen. Seventeen feels old, but not compared to her. I think she's thirty-one–the oldest person I know. Too old and used up to survive the journey through the mountains.

Fumes from the bleach in my hair drift and curl into my eyes. I shut them, briefly. My neck stings, burns. I clamp together my chattering teeth.

It took three crates of apples, twenty pounds of dried salmon, and a half-ball of twine to buy bleach. It represented a quarter of our remaining winter food stores.

My scalp itches. I swing my legs and grind fingernails against the underside of the wooden stool.

"Sit still!" Mother smacks my bare arm.

The heat of her slap is almost a relief in the cold drafty room. A small fire smolders in the pit at the centre of the dirt floor. None of us can spare time to tend it.

No one else knows our plan. It's difficult, but better to keep it a secret. Some of us try to earn favour with the porcine. Secrets in exchange for living a few more months, though I've never really understood the point. We know who the traitors are, and–worse it seems to me–they have to live with themselves.

I know it's harder for boys. For girls, successful breeding is a sure path to a longer life. I'm tagged for slaughter at eighteen, but the porky devils told me it could change to twenty or older, provided I keep producing viable children. They think they're providing an incentive to stay healthy. They are wrong.

My sister's tuneless hum overlays the snick and scrape of the saw blade. I want to block my ears so I can't hear her–so I don't have to think about her–but, of course, that's impossible.

"Can't you hurry it up?" My voice is thin and reedy. I clear my throat.

Mother ignores me.

The humming stops and singing starts.

I snap my head to the right, jamming the hacksaw blade into my neck. "Shut-up, Nessa. Mother can't concentrate." My voice rasps harsh and scared; I snap my mouth shut.

My ten-year-old sister squats under the window, pale hands on knees, fine blonde hair a curtain–the colour we are bleaching my mouse brown hair to. In the corner, a black spider spins a cocoon around a trapped fly.

"Look. Mary, it's so pretty." She peeks up at me, dimples showing.

"You're supposed to be watching the thermometer, Nessa." Mother's voice is gentler than I've heard in a long time.

Nessa's dimples disappear. She nods, climbs back onto the crate and leans out the window. "Down two degrees," she calls out. There's music in her voice even when she isn't singing.

My stomach churns. I straighten and stare straight ahead at my rumpled bed. Mother made a pink dye from fir bark and rubbed it around our eyes; I coughed and tossed in bed when the porcine came by.

The porcine are paranoid of illness. They wouldn't enter our hut and therefore took others with them into their cellars–hostages against the behaviour of the rest of us during the cold spell.

Warm blood trickles down the front of my chest and soaks into the coarse cloth of my shirt. I don't wipe at it. I've already interrupted Mother's work more than necessary.

The porcine track the location of all humans older than ten. Nessa turns eleven in five months. After that, she'll no longer be able to run errands for us. Neither Mother nor I dare go anywhere near the stash of weapons and tools we hid in a collapsed building on the south side of town. This winter is our last and best chance.

The porcine watch us, herd us, and try to keep us from harming ourselves. Many of us still find a way. The yokes contain a GPS tracking device embedded in the metal. It's the weakest part of the yoke–an ideal spot to cut through–but Mother needs to avoid damaging it.

Though scary, strong, and smart, the porcine don't have an affinity with technology. However, they always have a supply of the trackers and it's unlikely they found them in the abandoned and crumbling buildings of this former logging town.

Every few months, a plane flies overhead. It's our only sign an outside world remains. Sometimes containers fall onto the fields and the porcine collect them. They know they're coming.

There's only one conclusion that makes sense–the people across the mountains are supplying the porcine with the means to keep us enslaved.

Mother tells stories from a long time past about when humans risked beatings to build signal fires and write messages with rocks near the cliffs and on the beach every time they heard the sound of engines overhead. It took them a couple of years to realize the planes did not come to rescue them.

The porcine's only true enemy is the cold, an irony not lost on them or us. It's been many years since arrogant human fools played God in the name of leaner farm animals who could thrive outdoors in Alaska. At least they claimed that was the goal; Mother believes they were terrorists who lost control of the weapon they were creating. Among the humans, there are many theories. All we know for sure is their manipulations produced an intelligent, self-aware animal that didn't take kindly to being raised as food. Can't say I blame them.

My chest starts to tingle. Not now! I press my palms against my breasts. I've been careful to not let the porcine notice my youngest is almost weaned.

I have birthed two boys. Both are under three and cared for by older girls who have not begun their monthly bleed. Once they turn five, boys do physical work–chopping wood, carrying water, and digging. Boys are yoked at eight.

Males rarely turn sixteen; it depends on how quickly they reach puberty. With each generation they're a bit younger. My father was served up at seventeen. Mother keeps track in a little notebook stashed in a box buried in the dirt beneath her bed.

The sawing against my neck stops. I glance up.

Mother steps back. "This is taking too long." Her eyes narrow and she runs cold, bloody fingers between the yoke and my shredded skin.

# Mountains to Cross

"Ahh, it's thinning. Finally."

I brush my fingertips over the slick metal. The links and scrolls are thick and intricate. I like the idea they're being defaced.

Each of the fifteen porcine clans has its own blacksmiths and apprentices. They fight for the honour, great wallowing dust-ups that further scar their ugly pink and black hides.

I'm property of the Landtaw clan. Their blacksmiths are skilled at the forge. I wish they'd stick to forging gates and porcine jewelry.

The Chocbian clan own Mother. Their ham fists are only good for working thick, clunky iron–impossible to break with old, weathered tools.

Swarace clan's work is finely wrought and sought after by all the clans. They are the worst to belong to. They mark their property by fitting the yokes before they cool. Nessa is one of theirs.

Mother holds bolt cutters at an angle. I clench my teeth, knowing it's going to hurt.

"Tilt your head. There's not much room."

She slides the jaw of the cutters between the yoke and my skin. The pain is more than I expect, the moan something I can't keep in. My eyes water and I clutch the edge of the stool and drum my heels against the ground.

"It's done," Mother sounds matter-of-fact.

Nessa pats my shoulder and then clasps my hand, squeezing it.

I shake her off and help Mother peel away the yoke.

"Check the thermometer, Nessa," I growl.

"Down another degree," she chirps with a smile.

Mother lifts a bucket. Ice cold water drenches my head. Frothing bleach water soaks into the sandy dirt of the floor. I dry my hair with an old square of burlap, then drag a comb through it.

It's time.

I grab the pack at my feet and strap it on. There is a cape under the mattress of my bed. I roll it up and tuck it under my arm.

Nessa is flushed. She grins, tucks herself under Mother's arm and reaches up to hug her. Mother leans over awkwardly and closes her eyes.

They stand there, silent and still, and I want to throw up.

I try to soften my voice, but it splinters like broken glass. "Time to go, Nessa."

Mother nudges Nessa away. "Go, child."

Through moist lashes, Nessa stares at me. "We'll be back soon. Right, Mary?" she whispers.

I don't answer.

It takes me fifteen minutes to bike the backway to the edge of the town ruins. Nessa waits for me at the bottom of the hill. She's panting but bright-eyed.

I lift and hold her while I fasten around her waist the second strap we attached to the pack. The cape is as large as we could make it, and it barely wraps around both of us. I steady the bike and start pedalling.

The hill is steeper than it appears at a distance. The sun is out now, but we're still in shadow and it remains damn cold. Thankfully.

My thigh muscles burn with the effort of pushing the pedals, while the rest of me freezes. I don't look up. Those bald peaks have edged the horizon my entire life, and the plan is to never see them again.

Weed-streaked, rocky slopes arch away from deep ditches. Browned stalks of peppergrass edge the road. I know it's edible, though I've never tasted it. We are not allowed to keep any we forage. The porcine consider it a delicacy.

"How long, Mary?"

Her tiny figure hunches in front of me, and I resist the urge to snap. "Honey, we talked about this. Remember who's doing the work here and hush." I keep my voice low. Even though I know it's safe, my chest tightens. For reassurance, I glance at the thermometer now strapped to the handlebar. There's still a five-degree buffer, but I know it won't last.

The sun worries me. I have no idea what's beyond this hill or how far porcine territory extends.

Legs numb, I push harder. Stopping is certain death. Staying would've been the same–eventually.

One edge of the cape flaps out of my grasp. I snatch it back. Nessa sniffles.

My sister's size and trusting nature make her a good choice. Our mother's choice, but I agreed.

I press my arm against her for reassurance. "Don't worry, it'll be over soon and we'll both be free."

She shakes her head and straw-blonde hair gets in my mouth. I rearrange the cape to hide her hair. My stomach twists. I breathe in deep and exhale through my teeth.

Those I'm attempting to rejoin signed a treaty with the porcine. In the decades since, anyone who tries to escape is caught, killed, and consumed. The humans across the mountains abandoned us to this fate.

We are carriers of a mutated swine flu-like illness, deadly to the rest of humanity. Our only use is as food for the invaders. The porcine laugh at us, in that bone-shaking, guttural sound they make. We are spoils of war, but we can also be weapons.

I'm counting on it.

The rusty bicycle shakes and clanks. The chain hesitates in protest against the cold. I straighten my legs, stand taller, exhale a frosty mist and bear down on the pedals. Nessa squeaks as we crest the hill. I curve my body around her. We are one.

Shoulder-to-shoulder, hoary mountains guard the snaking road until it disappears into a distant bank of lowering clouds.

The chill air bites at my face as gravity takes over the work of moving us forward. The road is slippery. I stick my legs out to the sides, fight to control the handlebars, and steer around missing or heaved pavement. The strap holds Nessa against me or she'd tumble away. I'm not ready for that to happen.

When the deadly disease struck, they quarantined the entire state of Alaska. The mutated virus killed off the researchers who created the porcine, a few of their genetically-engineered monsters, and most of the rest of the remaining population.

The porcine took control of the state and it didn't go well for us.

The outside humans bombed Alaska, but they botched the job. A handful of porcine escaped and travelled down the coast well into Canada. They invaded, infected the population and enslaved the survivors–us. They threatened to cross the mountains and continue until humanity was decimated.

A treaty was signed. A treaty I intend to break.

The plants along the side of the road stir. They are too far away to be affected by the wake of our passing. Wind means I'm running out of time.

My newly bleached hair blows across my face. Over my shoulder, dark clouds chase us. I bend forward, tucking Nessa further under me.

Mother said my best chance is to reach the old forest where trees are taller and thicker–where surveillance cameras don't record everything.

I resist the urge to look for cameras. They're old. Hopefully the images of us won't be clear. Hopefully the outside humans haven't thought to replace them.

When temperatures dip this low, the porcine huddle around fires in the pits they call home. The stated goal of the researchers who created them was not reached. The porcine are not cold hardy, but neither am I.

The terrain flattens. Our momentum dissipates. I pedal past fields of brambles; a slumbering mahogany blanket shrouds the remains of a former mountain village. Perhaps that mound is a house, that one a car. Spiny blackberry canes clutch the edges of the pavement. Claiming. Reclaiming.

Nessa tries to point at something. I grab her arm and yelp at her to stay under the cape.

By now, Mother will have dropped my yoke into the sea. It was her idea to claim I slipped and fell while fishing. They rarely recover drowned bodies, or even try. The porcine aren't fond of the sea or fish, but they like the taste when we eat it, so they accept the occasional collateral reduction of the herd.

The swollen scars around my neck itch and burn. They will thicken as the new damage heals. Holding my head straight makes the jabs of pain worse, and I dare not rub the scars in case I lose control of the cape covering both of us.

The brambles give way to a rocky stream on one side. Hemlock and birch crowd the shore.

*Wait for the old forest*, Mother said, but I'm not sure how much longer I can pedal and control this ancient, cobbled-together bicycle.

In front of me, Nessa squirms. "I need to pee."

"It won't be long," I croon. "Then we'll stop."

A dusting of snow swirls in patterns around yawning potholes and buckled asphalt. Fine snowfall tells me the temperature has risen more than five degrees. The porcine will soon clamber out of their homes. I've run out of time.

The snow thickens–large flakes flutter past, attaching to each other. The clumps cling to Nessa's hair, my eyelashes.

Like sentinels, the trees of the forest loom in the distance. I pedal harder, my eyes narrowed to slits, my knuckles white.

Too soon we arrive–specks moving along a wilderness corridor.

"Hang on!" I yell. "Close your eyes."

Nessa curls into me. Her trust is a leaden weight in my gut.

I release one hand and tighten the other. The shaking of our bones, the rattling of metal parts, they are as one.

I am sentinel too. Detached.

I can do this.

My sister's hair is damp and soft under my hand. I smooth it back, knuckles grazing the back of her neck.

Twisting the handlebars, I aim for a spot where tree boughs overhang the road. I've practiced this, but never with the extra weight. It would've been cruel to let Nessa know her fate.

A flick of my wrist releases the strap that keeps her safe and hidden against me. My hand lifts and cups her chin.

Backward pedaling.

Braking hard.

Snap.

The bones are easy to break. I'm briefly surprised.

Airborne together. Her body hits the ground first, breaks my fall.

I roll away, toward cover. Under the trees, I gather myself together.

Mother warned me not to look back. I do anyway.

Through tangled blonde hair Nessa stares, her brown eyes wide and glazed. Around her, a yellow stain creeps across the snow.

I crawl back. It's a risk–we don't know exactly where the cameras are–but I can't make myself walk away.

My fingers close her eyes and leave red streaks across her cheeks, like war paint. I arrange the cloak over her like a blanket, a shroud.

Then I run, putting distance between me, my broken sister, and the bicycle in the ditch.

I'll be travelling through the mountains for months, maybe even years. I have the knowledge, if not the experience, to survive. No one on either side will search for me; I'm dead in the sea, and Nessa is dead in the mountains.

I'm looking forward to meeting those who live free. I hate them, probably more than I hate the porcine. They don't know what we sacrifice so they may live, but they're about to find out.

KT Wagner loves reading and writing speculative fiction. Occasionally she ventures out of her writers' cave to spend an hour or two blinking against the daylight, or reacquainting herself with family and friends. Several of her short stories are published and she is working on a sci-fi horror novel. She puts pen to paper in Maple Ridge, B.C., organizes Golden Ears Writers, and attended SFU's Southbank program in 2013 and The Writers' Studio (TWS) in 2015. KT can be found online at www.northernlightsgothic.com and @KT_Wagner

# The Reckoning

By M.J. Moores

## PRESENT

I hugged my body closer to the crumbling brickwork in a back alley of the old city. Pale snatches of frosty air escaped into the black night and multiplied as my breath kept time with the rapid beating of my heart.

Taking advantage of a new noon and the kind of dense shadow-work that only resonant light-pollution produced, I slipped around the corner and behind an industrial-sized trash bin. A blast, a bomb in slow motion, echoed as the fiery wake of the Second Launch to Mars lit the distant sky. Like billions of other people, I ignored the taunt.

A patrol drone hummed by, keeping to the main street. Its rotating strobe monitored the turf at 360 degrees on two axes, making the oversized Frisbee look like a miniature alien ship.

"Thank God it's green," I whispered.

Had it turned red, a silent alarm would've alerted the cops on patrol. To be safe, I waited another minute, trying to ignore the fact that my fate had sealed shut even before I was born. *Come on, get your head in the game, Angie.* I shook the old ache from my mind before hurrying to the end of the alley.

The metal door, painted to look like the surrounding brickwork, had no exterior handle. I pulled back the top portion of my mittens and licked an exposed finger. Smearing my saliva over a small rectangle of Plexiglas, where the handle should have been, I rubbed it off again with my jacket sleeve a second later.

A blast of frigid wind ricocheted down the long, narrow alley. I shivered and hitched up my collar before hiding my fingers again. It was anyone's guess how long the bio-recognition sequence would take—it was piecemeal tech at best. But really, what more could I expect from a black-market operation?

I crouched down to one side of the door, hugging my legs to my chest. Breathing hot air into the hollow my knees made, I warmed my face.

The Genesis rocket, little more than a shooting star now, brought thousands of *perfect* human beings to their new home. I ground my teeth then let them chatter, but only for a moment. I tried to keep my mind blank, focusing on the door and the open end of the alley, but each minute passed inside an eternity. Without fail, the neural chip at the top of my spinal cord pushed everything to the fore as my mind encased me once again in memory …

## 13 MONTHS, 10 DAYS AGO

The irregular but incessant beep and lack of smell told me I hadn't won the battle of bike vs. car. *Friggin' asshole, would-be driver.* It happened right at the cross-walk to the college too.

I remembered the weightlessness of being catapulted into the air, and the slow-motion dawning of the idiot talking into his headset while scrolling through something on the nav screen. I knew it wasn't a map or any standard function the system allowed. Just before my head smash into the upper windshield, reams of numbers slid by only to end in a multi-line graph.

I squeezed my eyes shut tighter, forcing the image away.

The persistent beeping made my skin crawl. I cracked an eye to locate the source of the sound. A white monitor sat next to my ear. Every time a spike crested the top of the screen, it beeped. I raised my hand to shove the monitor away, but my arm worked like taffy on a cold day. It didn't move right away and when it did lift, it felt twenty pounds heavier. Instead, I rotated my arm on the bed. It was covered in gauze bandages. *What the* … the words formed in my mind but not with my tongue.

"Angeline?"

I knew that voice. Cracking the other eye, I slowly turned my head.

"Angie, Honey! She's awake! Doctor Hathaway, she's awake!"

*Mom* … I tried to speak again but still my heavy tongue refused to move, my lips remained frozen and slightly parted.

A tentative pressure registered on my other hand. Nudging my head so gravity could drop my chin to my chest, I watched as Mom alternately squeezed and patted my near lifeless body part. But Mom wasn't looking at me. Her body remained half-turned toward an open door on the other side of the sterile room. My consciousness moved like sludge. I closed my eyes and passed out just as an insatiable itch fired along the nape of my neck …

**PRESENT**

The fake brick door disengaged and pushed opened with a hydraulic arm. I stood and slipped inside, hit the red button on the wall, and felt the door soundlessly whip shut. Low lighting guided my feet down the pitted concrete steps. I didn't rush, even if my new driving pulse demanded it.

I gave my arms a shake as the rubber on the soles of my shoes cloaked my descent. The roar of the rocket's engines disappeared with the shutting of the door. Seven trips over seven years and the rest of us would be left behind to face the Reckoning.

The lighting flickered. I'd grown used to being in dark places over the past year. Surprisingly though, the darkest one happened to be bright white and absent of scent …

**13 MONTHS, 9 DAYS AGO**

"No … You can't be serious." I raised my hand to touch the thin vertical scar at the base of my skull. A task easily done since they'd shaved my head for the surgery. I didn't actually touch it—I couldn't now that I knew what it was.

"Honey, you're alive. What does it matter if they used biotech? You're not paralyzed and the defibrillator didn't make your heart condition any worse. They're letting you come home in a few days."

Mom never had a problem with technological advances. The fact that I now had a piece of spinal cord made from someone else's dead baby made me heave. Mom snatched a plastic bedpan and shoved it under my chin. The puke hit the shallow tray and splattered all over the bedding and her arm.

A nurse helped Mom get everything cleaned up, but they served only liquids for dinner that night—the juice and chicken broth came back up too. That time I had a bucket nearby.

For two days I lay there as if comatose. I refused to do my exercises or acknowledge anyone who came to my room.

The image of a tiny foetus being extracted during a *legal* abortion kept replaying over and over in my head. The video they'd shown in sixth grade was supposed to delicately outline the new procedure for harvesting stem cells, growing new DNA compatible body parts, and attaching them to needy patients. But my brain just skipped past those parts. It showed me the minute, perfectly formed human, and then the new biochip tech used to help the body assimilate.

Dead baby.

Biochipped body part.

Dead baby.

Biochipped body part.

In the predawn hours on the morning of my release, I knew what I had to do.

The orderly found me in the midst of a seizure, lying across blood-splattered sheets, hemorrhaging from the gouge to the base of my skull. That genetic-atrocity was coming out no matter what …

## PRESENT

The shiny stainless steel door at the bottom of the stairs had no window; what it did have was a digital handle. I pressed the pad, mounted to the top of the pull, with my thumb and felt the air-tight seal disengage. I walked into a small antechamber. My eyes scanned the list of instructions projected onto the stainless-steel wall beside the door in front of me. The one behind me resealed.

The twitch in my right hand made it difficult to unbutton my coat. Manoeuvring the sweater over my head, the reflective metal walls taunted me with the image of an angry red scar dividing one breast from the other. For a moment, as I stood there in my bra and underwear, holding the little booties a drop-drawer had opened to reveal. I looked around, terrified. The shock, fear and anger I'd felt ten months ago crashed into every neuron. I hugged myself and trembled, waiting for the next set of instructions …

## 11 MONTHS, 7 DAYS AGO

Mother shoved me out of the car and locked the doors. I stumbled to catch my footing then backed up and flattened myself against the rounded contour of the electric model. There were no exterior door handles and the side-view mirrors had already retracted. *Nothing to grab on to.*

The heat from the sun-baked fibreglass penetrated the internal chill my weak heart exuded. Mother wore her no-nonsense face. We were done arguing, done crying ignorant tears. She grabbed my wrists and yanked me forward. I staggered, trying to lock my knees and stand my ground. It worked about as well as my logic for rejecting the offer of a new heart. It was bad enough the doctors had fixed whatever damage I'd caused with the scalpel that day, but now they wanted to fit me with a *biogenic* heart.

That particular muscle had been weak from birth, but I'd learned quickly how not to over-exert myself, live peacefully with the threat of a potential murmur and eventual extinction. The use of the defibrillator in the wake of my purification attempt left the already strained muscle damaged beyond repair. I still refused treatment. I'd deal with it the same way I always had.

Mom dragged me close and clamed an arm around my shoulders, still holding the wrist pinned between us in a death-grip. I'd been forced to spend six weeks in the psych ward until I was no longer a "threat to myself or others".

At home Mom fretted day and night for two weeks over every little choice I made. She drove us both insane with her relentless nattering about *absolutely having to get the surgery because a mother wasn't supposed to outlive her child.* I'd argued, used logic, emotion, begged *and* pleaded until I was hoarse; but the moment my mother forced me through the doors of Healing Waters, I gave up. This was never about what *I* wanted. Mom escorted me over to the woman at the reception desk.

"Hello. I'd like to admit my daughter, Angeline DuMont, for treatment."

"Certainly, Ms DuMont. What we offer is a reflective-based sharing program, where Angeline will work toward recovery on her own terms, without the use of prescription drugs to control temperament." The woman wore casual cotton pants and a blouse, but her demeanour oozed clinical efficiency.

"Your website mentioned a water therapy option. I'd like Angie to be placed in *that* program. She has a delicate heart and the doctors advised—"

"No need to get into all that, Ma'am. Here are the forms. Please make note of it there."

To me one rehab centre was the same as the next—they all worked to get you to believe something you didn't want to.

My mother dragged me over to a plush seating area. When we sat, she locked her ankle around mine. *Whatever.* I just sank back into the padded chair. My heart gave a flutter and my pulse quickened.

I did my breathing exercises as Mom filled out the paperwork. I decided then and there that I'd make full use of the water option thingy, but they'd never convince me to accept another piece of biotech.

And yet, twenty-eight days later I called my mother from the front desk.

"Hello?"

"It's me."

"How do you feel, honey?"

"Confused."

"Confused? Is that good or bad?"

"I don't know. Don't bother coming to get me. I'm signing myself in for another session."

"You are?" Mom sounded hopeful.

"I'll talk to ya next month."

"Oh, uh, that's it?"

"Bye, Mom."

"Bye, hon."

I scribbled my signature on the bottom line, the receptionist swiped my credit card and then took back all of my contraband items—most of which were still in the clear plastic box sitting on the counter between us: one watch, two rings, four bobby pins, a stick of gum, and my wallet. Then, I hurried down the "guest wing" to the meeting room at the far end. I didn't want to be late.

Leaning against the door, I paid the price for rushing. My body vibrated from the simple effort. Focusing on my breathing exercises, I listened through the thin pane of glass as Tony started the official introduction to the *reflective sharing* portion of the program.

When the light-headedness passed and I regained control of my legs, I clicked open the frosted Plexiglas door and slipped in. I sat between Quy and Louie, the only two "guests" I bothered to talk to on a regular basis. Only seven participants at this meeting—it was a *special* one. While I no longer saw these people as strangers, I'd never claim a true friendship with any of them. The mental baggage we carried made sure of that.

"And it looks like we can welcome back Angie," Tony said.

The others clapped politely.

"Since we're all familiar with this bi-weekly special invite, I'd like to open the floor to questions." Tony smiled. The thin white scar lining his right ear and the slightly thicker one trailing down his throat to his chest bespoke his first two transplants—I knew surgeons hadn't made those incisions and all Tony mentioned of his past was its darkness.

Most of those present leaned forward, resting arms on knees. The mix of eagerness and wariness would have made me laugh a month ago—but not now. Only Louie sat back with his arms crossed firmly over his chest. I remembered that pose well.

"How do we know you're not lying?" Louie started.

"What would I have to gain?" Tony asked.

"It could be a conspiracy for all I know. Maybe having three or more bits of biotech in us will turn us into government slaves instead of these Higher Humans you talk about."

The same thing niggled at the darker places in my mind too. There was still too much I didn't understand.

"It's against the law to have more than two pieces of biotech, you know that," Tony said. "If this *were* a conspiracy, wouldn't you expect the government to encourage biotechnology at every possibility, not restrict it?"

"But why us?" asked Quy. "Why are we the only ones who've been told about becoming Higher Humans?"

"Not everyone carries the genome variant that's able to biologically assimilate the tech cells now infused into the makeup of your new body parts. Out of the thirty-two people currently being assisted with accepting their biotech implants here, you seven carry the right alleles."

"But I was forced to accept my first bio implant," I said. "I don't agree with the technology. It's in humane." My hand slipped up the side of my neck to the raised vertical scar at the base of my skull, longer and thicker than it had been in its first inception. "Why would I go against my given right to refuse this treatment, and not only get a *new* heart but undergo surgery for a third biotech part I don't even need?"

Several of the others nodded in agreement. Every person sat there because they didn't want the tech in the first place. *Why would we willingly and illegally undergo three such surgeries? Why's it so important to keep us alive when there's no chance we'll be accepted into the Genesis Program?*

"In your case, Angie, replacing your heart with this technology will give you a better chance to live a long and healthy life free of breathing exercises, extreme caution, and confinement to mediocrity. The quality of your life *will* improve drastically."

"But the parts are grown from aborted foetal stem cells. You can't tell me you condone that shit?"

"Why are you so against the idea?" Marie asked. The robust dark-haired Columbian girl shifted to the edge of her seat. This was the first time she'd sided with Tony.

I felt myself slide forward. *Don't get up. Don't make a hostile move.* "Human life is sacred."

"Exactly," she said. "So, the League of Nations sanctioned *some* cases for abortion—not all. You and everyone else here know that not anyone can walk into a clinic and have their baby problem resolved. There's a screening process: underage victims of rape, mentally or physically disabled foetus' with low quality of life expectancy … children who would've lived a tortured life had they been born are helping those of us with better chances, to survive a bit longer in this crazy world."

"A *bit* is right." I couldn't keep the growing bitterness from my voice.

Nothing was clear anymore. I knew I'd never have children, it wouldn't be anything but a death sentence for them. It was the same argument used in the main meetings, but just because the world government *said* foetal stem cell research could happen, didn't make it right.

Tony took up the rally from Marie, "Now, knowing that, doesn't it make sense to enjoy every possible moment you have in good health?"

"I suppose."

That wrinkle between his brows told me he didn't believe me. I'd seen it often enough in the past month.

"Okay, Tony," Louis shot. "What about our kids, should we have any? Will *they* be guaranteed a life on the new Mars colony? Angie's heart problem is genetic. Will they suddenly accept her kids because they're Higher Humans? What if they're born after the last selection? What kind of future will they have being stuck on Earth when the Reckoning happens? We know for a fact that humans won't survive the next planetary change."

I nodded and sat up straight with my hands on my knees. *Yes. What does it all matter? This is why I came back. This is what I need to understand.* I'd accepted at an early age that my time would be finite—that'd I'd have no legacy after death. I believed what my mother told me, what the government fed us like baby Pablum: *Your life matters, even if it's short.*

"Unauthorized studies have proven that those of us with this chromosome variant, who have successfully assimilated *three* or more biotech body parts, change on a fundamental level." He paused. "The biotech not only works with our body, but takes on a kind of symbiosis integrating its neural network with our own. And we can pass both the gene variant *and* a portion of the biotech network in our bodies on to our children *naturally*—allowing us and them to live through and beyond the Reckoning, when everyone else will die."

Suddenly life after death seemed all too possible.

A month later I agreed to the biotech heart transplant. Three months after that, when my mother finally believed I was all right, I dropped out of college and got a job. Mom freaked, but accepted that I didn't want to waste what was left of my time studying for a job that might not exist after the last launch.

That's when I started following the underground connections Tony gave us for surgeons in the old city—once proud doctors now forced to work *off the grid* due to malpractice suits that spawned bankruptcy. Six months after that I got on the right list...

**PRESENT**

Another metal drawer dropped open containing hospital scrubs. I took them out and placed my clothes, coat and shoes in the now empty cavity and shuffled into the gear. The drawer shut. A green light in the upper-right corner of the room turned red. I jumped when the disinfecting mist spurted from retractable metal nozzles. I held my breath as long as possible. When the light turned green, I exhaled and coughed trying to catch my breath.

A panel door slid open across from me.

I stepped into the surgery theatre.

One half of my senses relaxed to see such a high-end operation: Two industrious nurses prepared for the surgery as Doctor Mohammed walked toward me; the other half of my senses exploded every nerve ending in my body, making my skin and eyes ache.

"Welcome, Miss DuMont. We're ready for you."

I didn't know what to say, so I just nodded and hugged myself as he led me over to the operating table, one metallic rail already lowered. I boosted myself onto the bed, a fake leather cushion, easily disinfected. My biotech heart slammed against the ribs caging it. After a lifetime of breathing exercises, I couldn't remember any.

One of the two nearly identical looking nurses helped me lie back. I thought for sure she'd feel my pulse racing, but she didn't say anything. The other nurse suspended a blue paper-like sheet over my body and up to my chin.

*Oh my God, this is happening!*

Then the flashes took over again:

Dead baby.

Biochipped body part.

Dead baby.

Biochipped body part.

I squeezed my eyes shut. Instead, I focused on the sound of Doctor Mohammed's voice during last week's consultation in an upper city rent-an-office: *I'll simply remove your old appendix and replace it with the biotech one we'll grow for you this week.*

"Open your mouth please," Nurse One said.

I opened my mouth and my eyes. The nurse swabbed my cheek then touched it to a hand-held DNA reader. A white light at the top of the reader flashed three times. She nodded to the doctor.

"We have a perfect match, Miss DuMont," he said.

My palms grew damp. A trickle of sweat dripped into my eye from the heat of the bright overhead lamp. I blinked, mouthing words I couldn't articulate. *Am I really going to do this? A repaired spinal cord, a new heart, and a body part that might kill me anyway if it happens to rupture for God knows what reason? For what? An unsubstantiated truth? Potentially forged research results and the Hail-Mary that life, my life, could exist after the Reckoning?*

"Are you ready, my dear? You need only say the word and we can cancel the surgery."

*Is that even an option now?* I'd paid for the tech, I'd paid for his time, I'd depleted my college fund, and for what?

## The Reckoning

Nurse Two repositioned the bright white light over my stomach. Red spots flashed in my eyes. Nurse One attached a heart monitor to my finger.

Beep, beep. Beep, beep. Beep, beep. Beep, beep, beep. Beep, beep, beep—

"Are you ready to initiate *the change*?"

Nurse One held up a large needle full of some kind of anesthetic.

Nurse Two lifted a scalpel from a metal tray.

I held my breath and closed my eyes, scrunching my hands into fists under the sheet.

*Am I?*

MJ Moores began her career as an English teacher in Ontario, Canada. She relishes tales of adventure and journeys of self-realization. MJ is an author, small press editor, freelance writer for Authors Publish Magazine, Indyfest Magazine, and she runs the emerging writers website Infinite Pathways. Be sure to check out her sci/fi fantasy series, The Chronicles of Xannia.

Connect with MJ at:
http://mjmoores.com or http://facebook.com/AuthorMJMoores

# A Note from the Publisher

Unbound II – Changed Worlds, is our second in the Unbound anthology. Thank you for purchasing your copy and supporting all the great authors who work tirelessly to bring fantastic stories to you.

In order for us to continue bringing you such great works of fiction we need your help. Please visit Goodreads and/or Amazon or any book outlet you purchased it from and leave a rating. Your honest feedback will help others find the edition.

If you enjoyed this edition, you may also enjoy the prior Unbound I – Lost Friends, and our upcoming version, Unbound III – Broken Chains.

Find out more about our books and authors at:

https://scififantasypublications.com

or visit our publication site:

https://daowenpublications.ca

www.ingramcontent.com/pod-product-compliance
Lightning Source LLC
Chambersburg PA
CBHW051239170626
46809CB00004B/1401

* 9 7 8 1 9 2 8 0 9 4 2 1 0 *